FATAL SECRET

M.L. ROSE

This is a work of fiction. Names, characters, businesses, places, events and incidents are either the products of the author's imagination or used in a fictitious manner. Any resemblance to actual persons, living or dead, or actual events is purely coincidental.

Copyright © ML Rose, 2025

The moral right of the author has been asserted.

All rights reserved. No part of this book may be reproduced or used in any manner without the prior written permission of the copyright owner. This prohibition includes, but is not limited to, any reproduction or use for the purpose of training artificial intelligence technologies or systems.

To request permissions, contact the publisher at rights@stormpublishing.co

Ebook ISBN: 978-1-80508-342-9
Paperback ISBN: 978-1-80508-344-3

Cover design: Sara Simpson
Cover images: Shutterstock

Published by Storm Publishing.
For further information, visit:
www.stormpublishing.co

ALSO BY M.L. ROSE

Detective Nikki Gill Series
Stolen Souls
Silent Girl

ONE

Panic thudded in Chloe's chest, sending her heart rate surging. She turned, looked behind her for the man who had followed her into the club. She could see him everywhere, even when she was talking to her friends, and yet... And yet now she couldn't. She'd told her friends, but they couldn't see him. How could they not? He'd been right there, with his slightly hunched back, white beard, and gleaming eyes. Out of place. Old.

Chloe had run, trying to get as far as she could from him. She clambered into a cab, ignoring all the things she'd heard about getting into one alone. The driver looked at her in the mirror.

"Hollywell Street – please."

As he drove, she kept twisting in her seat, checking the other cars on the road. Nothing... He wasn't there. But why did she feel like he was?

Chloe jumped out of the taxi and paid the driver. She kept her face down and walked past the students enjoying their last few days of drunken bliss before they went home for the summer holidays. She darted a look over her shoulder and towards the dark shadows in the closed shops. No one was following her.

She thought about what he had said about her mother. Could it be true?

He had given her that piece of paper, which she could still feel in her pocket. She remembered the name.

DI Nikki Gill.

Tomorrow, Chloe would call her. She needed answers, and DI Nikki Gill might have them.

Chloe walked through the gates of New College, past the porters' lodge. Then she froze. Behind the glass window of the lodge was a man with a white beard.

Was it him?

Fear sprang like a tidal wave in her spine, overcoming her senses. She ran into the college, past the halls, out of the quad and into the vast rear gardens where students weren't allowed at night. Right now, she didn't care.

Chloe hid behind a tree, trying to calm her frenetic pulse rate. It was no use. Breathlessness clawed her lungs, hurting her chest.

Someone ran into the gardens, and Chloe drew herself back. When she looked again, she recognised the figure. Fiona. Chloe seethed inside. The lying bitch. Pretending to be her friend but chatting up Mark behind Chloe's back. A strange feeling fluttered in her chest. Was she working with the old man?

Chloe came out of the shadows.

Fiona stopped when she saw her. "Chloe! You left the club so suddenly. Are you okay?"

"No. Did you see that old man?"

Fiona got closer. She frowned. "No. What old man?"

Chloe looked around her, the trees and bushes forming threatening, dark shadows.

"Don't trust anyone," she whispered to Fiona. "He's coming after me."

In the distance, more people came into the grounds. Chloe turned and ran. Fiona shouted, calling Chloe's name out behind her.

Chloe found herself at the top of the ramparts and climbed over the single chain barrier that forbade entry. She felt herself propelled forwards, as if borne by the wind.

She heard a rustling sound and startled, then saw a bird settle on the rampart wall.

The crow turned its head, looking at her. Its black eyes gleamed and the moonlight shone on its dark feathers. What did it want?

Chloe waved her hands. "Shoo!" As she did, the bird flew away, a silver-black dart against the sky.

Below, a figure in the darkened gardens circled. Calling her name.

She needed to get as far away from it as possible. As far away from people. Chloe ran along the long rampart until she couldn't hear the voices. Couldn't see anyone. She was completely alone.

She reached a ruined tower, and with a flap of wings, the crow appeared again. It had come to find her.

Chloe stared at it. It was beautiful. She felt compelled to step closer, wanting to touch the creature. To feel the smooth black down on its head. As she tried to climb up the steps to reach it, she stumbled and some rubble loosened and fell, hitting the ground far below.

She held out a hand to touch the bird. The creature stood still, its glinting eyes fixed on her. The wind was stronger now, carrying her forward. With the next gust, the crow spread its wings and flew away.

"No!" Chloe cried out. She lunged after it and lost her footing. Her body lurched, and suddenly she was falling. A terrifying scream erupted from her lungs. Her fingers clawed on the ancient stone walls; nails ripped as she fought to find some purchase. Her body lost the fight with gravity. Chloe screamed again, the echo of her terror ripping into the silence of the night.

TWO

Detective Inspector Nikki Gill heard the alarm beeping and tried her best to ignore it. The incessant buzzing cut through her slumber, finally piercing the thin veil between dreams and wakefulness. She stretched out a hand and slapped the alarm. The offending machine tumbled to the floor, knocking over a bottle of water. Sighing, Nikki got up.

Last night the pub drinks had carried on for longer than expected. Nikki and her team had just caught the boss of an organised crime network operating out of Oxford, the result of a one-year surveillance operation.

Nikki trudged to the bathroom. When she looked at herself in the mirror, she grimaced. She hadn't taken off her makeup, and had just collapsed into bed. As she splashed water onto her face, she thought about her colleague Detective Inspector Monty Sen. He'd dropped her home and they had almost kissed on her doorstep. She felt a warm rush as she thought of the moment. She knew he wanted to, and so did she. But Monty was also a colleague, and she didn't want that complication in the workplace.

He knew everything about her now. Her troubled childhood in Oxford, and the tragic death of her brother, Tommy. Monty had kept her confidence, and Nikki knew no one else knew about it. She liked him for that. His lean, craggy, handsome face floated into her mind, and her heart jolted as she remembered the mischief in his eyes. She hadn't felt like that about a man for a long time. Nikki sighed and stepped into the shower. The old song about washing a man out of her hair came to her head. She did wash her hair, and perhaps she needed to wash out her feelings about Monty as well. But once she was showered and had wrapped a towel around her head, the thoughts of Monty were harder to dislodge.

As she put on her white shirt and blue blazer, her phone beeped. She had two missed calls from Nish Bhatt, one of her detective constables. She called him back, putting him on loudspeaker as she got ready.

"Good morning, guv. Sorry to bother you so early." Nish's normally cheerful voice was subdued, and he lapsed into silence. Nikki felt a strange tightening in her guts, a premonition of bad news.

"What is it?"

"A student fell to her death from New College walls. It happened last night; the college groundsman discovered the body this morning."

Nikki sat down on the bed. "Accident?"

"Uniforms say there are no obvious wounds or injuries from what they can see. They haven't touched the body, obviously. Perimeter's been set up and the crime scene's secure."

Nikki chewed her lower lip. It was unusual for a student to fall from the college walls. Was she climbing at night? Drunk? Some male students did foolhardy bets like that, and some got injured. But falling to death was new.

"Was there a party at New College last night?"

"No, according to the groundsman, and the porters' lodge.

I've reached out to the college warden, but haven't heard back as yet."

"Alright, call them again. I take it we have an ID on the student?"

"Not as yet. The groundsman recognises her vaguely, so do the porters. She lived in the college premises, they think. They can't recall her name, but it won't take long to get an ID."

"Sooner the better. I'm on the way, see you at the scene."

"Copy that, guv."

Nikki got ready quickly, taking her warrant card and extendable baton. She went swiftly downstairs. Her little thatched cottage was charming – just what she needed. It was small, but with two nice bedrooms upstairs. The narrow wooden stairs creaked under her feet. She had to watch her head as the wooden beam on the stairs landing was low, and she had bumped her head on it on more than once occasion.

She took a packed lunch and got into her car. It was the fourth of June. The sun was behind clouds, and mist was lifting slowly off the canal. Nikki liked living in Kidlington. She had grown up in Oxford, and knew the surrounding areas well. Kidlington was less busy than Oxford, and she enjoyed the quietness. As she started driving, she realised she hadn't spoken to her mother, Clarissa, in a week. Work had taken over. It was too early to call now; she'd make some time at lunch.

The drive to New College took a while in the morning rush hour. Trinity, or the summer term in Oxford, was still drawing to a close, and the colleges were full of students. Soon they would be gone, ready to start their summer vacations. As Nikki drove through the traffic, she remembered those heady days of her youth. She had got out of Oxford as soon as she could and gone to university in Durham. Her troubled home life had been torture, and she couldn't wait to get away. Now, all of it seemed so long ago.

The traffic got thicker when Nikki came off Banbury Road

and entered Oxford's main streets. Academics in suits were rushing to work, along with students. But there was also a crowd of labourers and the staff of the supermarkets and cafés that dotted Oxford's High Street. Oxford was a small town, and apart from the colleges it maintained a parochial outlook. Beyond the students, and the old money of the colleges, there lay a seedy town with a dark underbelly.

As she got closer to the college, Nikki felt the seediness in Oxford had got worse with time. The shiny new buildings and constant redeveloping was offset by the uptick in poor accommodation and crime. Old money stayed within the mute walls of the colleges.

In most Oxford colleges, the entrance was by foot, guarded by the porters' lodge. Vehicular access was separate. New College was different in that respect, as both humans and machines had a common entrance. Nikki drove slowly down Holywell Street, and noted the two uniformed sergeants standing outside the gates of New College. They were chatting to two men, one in a porter's uniform, the other a Police Community Support Officer, identifiable by his blue uniform and the words PCSO written boldly across his jacket.

They saw Nikki, and waved her in. Nikki went in slowly through the cobbled stoned entrance and saw the grey walls encircling, and hiding, the college from view. She felt like she was in a medieval castle.

She had been to New College once, many years ago, when Clarissa had wanted her to apply. Nikki couldn't think of anything worse than spending her university years in sodding Oxford. Where others saw magnificent architecture, she saw drab familiarity. It only bred contempt. But she had trudged along for the college visit day. The grey rampart walls had struck her as foreboding. Apparently, during the English Civil War, one of the college fellows had been a leading light for the Royalists and had stored weapons within the college walls. Hence the ramparts. The original college was built in 1379.

New College was built like a medieval fortress, its stone defensive ramparts – which had narrow slits to thrust spears through – surrounding the inner college grounds. Widely acknowledged as one of Oxford's oldest colleges, it was built by priests, who hid their treasures within the college grounds.

One of the uniformed sergeants she had seen hurried up to her, along with the PCSO. The sergeant was called Bradley, and he nodded at her.

"Morning, marm." He held out the customary clipboard where Nikki signed her name and rank.

Bradley was shorter than Nikki's five feet nine inches. He was a veteran of the Thames Valley Police, and good at his job. The brown-haired thirty-something cleared his throat before he spoke.

"IC1 female found by the college groundsman this morning. We're still waiting for a positive ID. It's likely that she's a college student, as she either had a pass, or lived in the residential halls." His face fell. "She's young, guv. No more than twenty, I'd say."

Nikki ground her jaws together. It was the second time she'd been called out for the death of a student. It wasn't nice, and she hoped this would be the last time.

"She could also have been invited. Just because she was found here doesn't mean she's a student at the college. She could be from another college, or from town. Or anyone. Keep an open mind."

Bradley nodded. "Yes, marm."

Nikki turned her attention to the PCSO. He was an older man, hair whitening and thin at the top. His slate grey eyes were appraising her. Nikki met the man's intense gaze, noting the sharp nose, the wrinkles on his forehead and around his eyes. There was a firmness in his jaws, and an intent in his expression. He was clean shaven. He stood slightly hunched, arms clasped behind a broad back. Despite his age, he was in good shape.

"And you are?" Nikki asked.

"PCSO Jason Arnett," the man said. He smiled, the deep crow's feet in the corner of his eyes crinkling. He didn't offer his hand, and Nikki appreciated that. PCSOs were junior staff, helping out the uniforms. "I'm assisting Sergeant Bradley."

"DI Gill." Nikki nodded her greeting.

Jason said, "The porters said they heard noises inside the quadrangle last night. There was no designated party or social event. It's possible the students had an impromptu gathering."

Nikki angled her eyes at Bradley, who was staring at Jason. Clearly, Bradley didn't know about this.

"You spoke to the porters?" she asked Jason.

"Yes. They went in to check but didn't find anyone. Not sure how hard they looked, given it was late at night."

Nikki considered Jason's words, and the man himself. He was proving to be useful already. The knack of speaking to people, and extracting information, was a good quality in a policeman.

"What time did the porters look?" Nikki asked.

"About one in the morning, the man said. His name's Dooley." Jason pointed at the glass box of the porters' lodge, where two men in black uniforms sat watching them.

"Did he say anything else?"

"Not much, no. Dooley wandered inside the quadrangle greens with his flashlight. He heard some sounds, like doors opening, and shoes on stone. But he didn't actually see anyone."

Bradley added, "And that was it until this morning, when the college groundsman did his rounds." It was a statement, not a question.

"That's what Dooley told me," Jason said.

"And where is the groundsman?"

Bradley answered. "By the crime scene, getting questioned by DC Young." That would be Kristy, the second detective constable in Nikki's team.

"DC Bhatt's also there," Bradley said.

"I'll head over. Good work," Nikki said, her eyes lingering on Jason. "How long have you been a PCSO?" She wondered what he had done with his life, and why he'd joined up now.

"Three months now. I'm retired from my security job. I used to work in Birmingham, for a supermarket chain. This is a good way to while away my time – and earn some money."

"Good for you." Nikki smiled at him. She liked Jason's initiative, when he should be enjoying the comforts of retirement. She bid them goodbye and followed Bradley's direction to the left of the walls. She could only describe them as castle walls, given the towers and ramparts. They were obviously not as high as a true castle, but they were tall enough to cause serious injury if someone fell.

Nikki walked around the corner, where the undergrowth was thicker, with trees leaning overhead. There was a path running through and, straight ahead, she could see a cluster of uniforms and the blue and white tape that was draped across the crime scene. A white Scene of Crime tent was being erected.

As she approached, she spotted the blonde curls of DC Kristy Young and the wide shoulders of DC Nish Bhatt, both with their backs to her. They stood separate from the group of uniforms, speaking in low voices to a nervous-looking man wearing overalls.

Kristy sensed Nikki and turned. Her lips stretched in a tight smile. "Hello, guv."

THREE

"This is John Lynes, the groundsman," Kristy introduced the man. He was old, and in his late sixties or seventies, Nikki thought, with the tanned face and arms of a man who spent his summers outdoors. His eyes were wide and he licked his lips as he stared at Nikki. It was clear he realised she was in charge. He rubbed the light stubble on his cheeks.

"DI Gill," Nikki said, holding up her warrant card. John didn't bother looking, he just stared at her.

"Tell us what you saw."

The groundsman's Adam's apple bobbed up and down. He wiped a hand over his sweaty forehead.

"Uh... I was out on my morning rounds about seven a.m. I generally start on the outside, then work my way in. If the porters have something outside, I tend to that as well. But first I go around the ramparts, just to check. That's when I came across..." His words died as he indicated the white tent.

"Be specific," Nikki said gently, aware the man was disturbed by his discovery. She couldn't blame him. "What did you see first?"

"The feet, sticking out of the bushes. She had trainers on.

Black, they were. Then I saw the legs, and the rest of the body. She lay on her front, not moving at all. Like, nothing. I got closer and called out. She didn't move. I nudged her legs with my foot. I knew then she was dead."

"Was she clothed? Did you see any blood? Or anything else around the body?"

"Yes, she was fully clothed. Nothing around her. I mean, I was too shocked to look properly. But nothing obvious. I called 999. Then the porters on my walkie-talkie. Yes, she had clothes on. Blue jeans, and a dark jacket."

Nikki persisted. "You saw nothing else around the body?"

John stared at her, then his eyes flickered to the ground. His cheeks were sunken, eyes hollow.

"Nope."

Nikki watched him for a few seconds. Not for a moment was she going to discount him as a suspect. Dangerous individuals had a flair for acting. They had extremes of emotion, and killers often showed genuine sorrow after the victim's death. The so-called malignant narcissistic personality disorder.

"You stayed here until the porters and then the police arrived?"

"Yes."

"How long have you worked here?"

John blinked a couple of times. "For the last two years. I've got a contract with the college. I manage a team of two people."

"You've never seen the victim?"

"To be honest, I hardly got a look at the face. She was lying face down like I said."

Nikki observed the man, not missing his thick, gnarled fingers, stained with nicotine. A working man's hand. He gripped a black cap in his hands. His shoes were scuffed with use. He shifted on his feet, aware that she was checking him out. Nikki noticed his left shoe was bigger than the right, and he tended to favour his right foot to stand. The heel on the left shoe was also thicker.

"Where did you work before?"

"I was a plumber. Gas safety engineer. Too much work to do the exams and that, so I packed it in. Became a landscape gardener."

"We will need an official statement from you. What time did you find the body again?"

"About seven-thirty a.m. I ran to the porters' lodge, and they called the police."

Nikki pursed her lips. "Okay. Hang around if you don't mind. We might need to speak to you later."

"I've got my office opposite the porters' lodge. I'll be there if you need me."

John left, and Nikki watched him walk away. Then she turned to her constables. "Has Dr Raman arrived?"

"She's on her way. Tom's dropping his kids off to school. He should be here soon."

Thomas Armstrong, or Tom, was a detective sergeant. After Nikki and Monty, he was the most senior person on the team. He was going through a divorce and had taken time off work but had recently returned on a part-time basis.

"Okay, let's go and have a look at the body. Have we put the college under lockdown?"

The two constables looked at each other and Nikki knew the answer. "One of you, inform the porters' lodge and security – no student or staff is allowed to leave the premises until we say so."

"Got it, guv," Nish said, and walked off quickly. Nish rang her boss, Detective Superintendent Dean Patmore. The DSU's gruff, twenty-a-day cigarette-smoker's voice came down the line.

"I heard. Are you on scene?"

"Yes sir. At New College, on Holywell Street. I'm going to

be the senior investigating officer on this case, is that correct? I'm first on scene."

"Yes, go ahead." He paused. "I'm going to inform the college warden, and the university chancellor. We will have media attention on this. It's probably on social media already."

"It might well be, sir. But we'll keep a lid on the crime scene, don't worry. I'll report to you at midday."

Nikki hung up. "Where's DI Sen?" she asked as they walked towards the white tent.

"Did someone say my name?" a voice called out behind them. Nikki stopped and half turned. The tall, lanky figure of Monty Sen was striding up the path with purpose. His black hair was swept back with gel, and his chestnut brown eyes danced with mischief. His brown skin was smooth and taut over his broad forehead. He was sporting a light beard that was a new addition to his face. Nikki tried not to stare, but Monty was more than pleasing on the eyes, and she had to admit the beard looked good on him.

Monty stopped and looked at both her and Kristy. Nikki blinked, and then realised she was blushing as Monty smiled at her. She glanced down quickly.

"Was it you, by any chance, DI Gill?" Monty's tone was deliberately playful. She wished he wouldn't do that – and she also wished like hell she could stop the heat on her cheeks.

"What time do you call this?" she demanded, raising an eyebrow. Memories of last night surfaced again. How she had almost leaned into his kiss but withdrew at the last second.

"I wanted you to take the lead." Monty grinned. "Isn't that what you want?"

He had seen through her. Nikki had fought hard to get to inspector grade, which was still not easy to achieve for a woman. At work, she had remained fiercely competitive. She was aware Kristy was following their conversation, which was now getting personal.

"Patmore just confirmed I'm the SIO," Nikki said, walking towards the white tent.

"Of course he did," Monty replied easily.

She glanced at him, but the smile on his face was genuine. He was a man without an ego, and she loved that about him. Despite his experience, he had not seen her as a rival when she'd joined the Thames Valley Police from the London Met. Which is exactly what she had expected him to do. All her male colleagues had been the same – bitter rivals who couldn't stand seeing a woman get the job before them. Monty was different.

They got to the white tent and a purple Tyvek-suited figure came out, lifting a flap. Jeremy, the assistant to Hetty Barfield, the head of SOC, lowered his mask.

"Hi. I'm just getting started. Lights all set up. Please step on the boards only if you can."

"Right," Nikki said. She mentally prepared herself for the scene inside. Despite her years of experience, seeing a dead body remained an emotive experience to Nikki. Yes, she was clinical and detached in her crime scene appraisal. But as a human being, she couldn't separate her feelings from her job.

She took a deep breath, and stepped inside.

FOUR

The woman lay on her belly, face down, her right eye and side of her face just visible. The undergrowth had been cleared where she lay, and bits of leaves and twigs had fallen on the victim's hair. Her brown hair lay like a halo over the damp green earth. Darkening blood had seeped under the hair and mingled with the grass. Her head had hit the side of a rock, damaging the left side of her skull. Her right eye was open, lips parted as if she was frozen in eternal shock.

Nikki went forward, stepping carefully on the sterile duck boards. She crouched by the woman's head, taking care not to disturb the white circles that the scene of crime officer had made, where evidence lay as yet uncollected. She saw drops of blood, and wisps of hair. There would be more samples, like skin cells, invisible to the naked eye.

Nikki felt the woman's cheek. It was ice cold and blanched white, and Nikki thought it was lower than the current ambient temperature. That coldness, or *algor mortis*, indicated death had occurred a good few hours ago. Body temperature decreased by one degree per hour in a dead body, on average, allowing for body size, presence of water nearby, and other factors.

A yellow discolouration was starting to seep into the skin. Nikki wasn't a pathologist, but she knew about *livor mortis*, the purplish grey colour that affected the skin from about half an hour post death, but took twelve hours to become fixed. That fixation had not happened as yet. Hence, death couldn't have been at eight last night, given that it was eight forty-five in the morning now.

Nikki looked carefully at the exposed right side of the face. No moles or other identifying marks. The left side, on the ground, had been battered by the impact of the fall. She knew the cheekbone would be fractured, causing bleeding into the sinus and eye sockets.

She pulled the earlobe to look behind it but didn't see any bruise or injuries. She noted the gold earring – a stud with a white stone in it. It looked expensive. The victim wore a necklace too, and slowly Nikki lifted the chain with a pen from her pocket. The chain and necklace were both intact. She knew SOCO would bag it as evidence, but she asked Monty to take a photo of the necklace, and he obliged.

The necklace was a gold cross, and the chain was also gold. The cross had white, precious stones, the same as those in the earring, embedded on both sides. Nikki wondered if they were diamonds.

She raised the victim's hair to look at the back of her neck. There was some bruising here, blood collecting on the left side, and the cervical spine or neck had probably snapped in a couple of places. Nikki's jaws tightened as her nostrils flared. It was never easy to be clinical, coldly collecting facts. She had done this job for twenty-five years, and this part was always difficult.

She straightened and crossed over to the other side of the body. Monty took her place, his sharp eyes roaming over the surroundings, then coming to a rest on the woman's coat pockets.

"What's that in her right-side pocket?" he asked, pointing.

Nikki looked at the woman's coat. The right pocket was visible, but she didn't see anything unusual.

She was about to ask Monty to explain when she noticed the difference. A casual observer would've missed it. A tiny paper fragment peeking out from the pocket. The paper was brownish, the same colour as the coat. It was easy to miss, but Monty clearly had eagle eyes.

Nikki pulled out the piece of paper with her gloved hand. The words were written in ink, in black capital letters. At first, they didn't make any sense to Nikki, but as she read it for the second time, her breathing got ragged, and a hollow sensation spread across her chest.

Ask DI Nikki Gill what happened.

It was there in black and white. There was no mistaking it. Nikki's mouth dropped open, her body frozen in shock. She was transfixed by the paper, her eyes drilling into the crumpled note. She felt Monty touch her arm. Without a word, she slowly turned her neck. His eyes were alive, burning, troubled.

"Let's go outside," he whispered. Nikki noted they were still the only ones in the tent. But any minute now, Jeremy the SOC technician would come back, as would Dr Raman.

Nikki didn't know what to do. Her shocked brain couldn't form a thought, think of a word. She accepted Monty's gloved hand like it was a lifeline in a stormy sea, and she was drowning in it. Stiffly, she got to her feet. She watched in dumb despair as Monty bagged the evidence and put it into his pocket to file with SOC. She had no intention of hiding it, in any case. Monty pulled her arm gently, and she followed him out of the tent.

FIVE

"What's it looking like, guv?" Kristy asked. Nikki avoided the constable's eyes and made a show of taking her gloves off. Monty was next to her, doing the same.

"No sign of trauma apart from the injuries from the fall." Nikki forced herself to speak. "But we need to examine the rest of the body. Best to wait till Dr Raman arrives."

Nikki felt like she was having an out-of-body experience. She was watching herself utter the words, standing somewhere else. Her brain seemed made of ice, all thoughts congealed into a frozen mass.

"Okay," Kristy said, and Nikki could tell the constable knew something was wrong. Over the last few months she had grown close to Kristy. She was wiser than her young years.

"Can I have a look inside?"

"Yes, of course." Nikki stepped to one side. She walked with Monty, further away from the white tent and the staff. Her brain was starting to work again, the shock slowly receding, replaced by the slow crawl of incredulity.

She looked up at Monty's face. His brown eyes were dulled with confusion, but she didn't see any judgement there. She could also read the questions in his expression, and he didn't have to utter the words. Her eyes snapped shut, and she rocked back on her heels.

"No," she whispered, then gripped her forehead. She put her hand down quickly, aware that the others might be watching her. Self-consciously, she glanced to her right, where the staff were busy by the white tent. To her relief, no one was looking in their direction.

"No," she repeated, holding Monty's eyes. "I didn't know that girl, and I have no idea what this is about. I mean, what the actual fuck? What the hell is this?"

Monty was still silent, and she didn't like that. He averted his eyes and pressed his lips together. He shook his head.

"The note said 'DI Nikki Gill'. Not Nikki, or Miss Gill. Someone knows you professionally. Or at least knows where you work and in what position."

"And they're trying to frame me? Or get me..." Words failed her again, as the confusion surged back.

"Into trouble," Monty finished for her. "They knew you would be examining the body. Well, who had access to the body before us?"

She looked at him, and he answered his own question.

"The groundsman, clearly. He would have had time to put the note into the victim's pocket. Or if the porters came to see the body, then it could have been one of them."

"But why? How do any of them even know who I am, or that I might be here?"

"They didn't have to know you would be here. They just wanted to get you into trouble."

Another thought struck Nikki. The uniforms had also been here, so had the new PCSO. It was an unpalatable thought, but she had to consider an internal culprit. When she mentioned it to Monty, he nodded grimly.

"The thought did cross my mind. But only the first uniforms

in place saw the body. They didn't allow anyone near it – and they didn't touch the victim. I spoke to Sergeant Bradley on my way up here." Monty's jaws hardened. "He's a good man. I trust him."

Monty's word was good enough for Nikki. She needed to stick to the facts, and hopefully the fog in her mind would clear.

"So, the uniforms didn't touch the body. They set up the perimeter, and informed Kristy and Nish. Then they called me."

"Yes," Monty confirmed. "Kristy called me, while I believe Nish spoke to you." He smiled. "You look good, considering the hangover."

His attempt to crack a joke was meant to lighten the mood, but Nikki wasn't feeling up to it. Besides, she did have a bloody hangover. She had popped a couple of paracetamols before she left home. The pressure on the sides of her temples was returning, gathering force in the middle. It felt like a drilling machine was working on her forehead, and her convoluted thoughts were making the noise worse. She massaged the corner of her forehead.

"Regardless, we need to ask the uniforms, and anyone else, if they moved or tampered with the body. Would you mind?"

Monty stared at her for a few seconds, seemingly to understand if she was getting paranoid. Or she thought so any way. Then he nodded and walked away. Nikki watched him go, wondering what he was thinking about her actions. But she needed to be thorough. The shock was receding slowly, leaving a bitter taste in her mouth.

She would have to declare their finding to Patmore, and he would launch a full investigation into her – aided by the Professional Standards Committee – the watchdog charged with the conduct of police staff. Nikki wasn't looking forward to it, but she had no choice. She knew Patmore didn't have any options either – it was always difficult when there was even the slightest whiff of corruption in the force.

Nikki groaned. She hoped like hell the Anti-Corruption Unit wouldn't get involved. She ground her teeth and looked around her. She needed to take control, and sort this out.

Across the grass verge, the rampart rose grey and foreboding in front of her. She walked back to the white tent, and to Kristy and Nish, who stood there chatting.

"Any ID?" Nikki asked the constables.

Nish replied, "Not yet, but I got hold of the college warden. He's assured me no one on site will leave the premises without his knowledge. But he can't guarantee the students won't find ways to leave." Nish gestured at the college. "The grounds are big. There's a chapel, a choir, offices, student and staff accommodation. It backs all the way to the High Street."

"Yes, I gathered. Like all Oxford colleges, they're designed to be self-sufficient." Nikki pressed her lips together. "It's Magdalene College, and the bridge over the Cherwell on the High Street, isn't it? At the back of the grounds, I mean."

"That's right, guv," Nish said.

"Ask uniforms to guard all the rear and side exits," Nikki instructed.

From her rudimentary knowledge of the Oxford colleges, she knew there would be paths that sneaked out into the main roads, often hidden from the casual observer. And that there were underground tunnels that led from the wine cellars and chapel basements and out through the sewers. More folklore than fact, though many Oxonians vouched for their presence. She couldn't stop everyone, but she had to try to interview as many students as she could.

"Where is the college warden? I need to speak to him. Get more uniforms on board. I'll call Patmore and get clearance."

SIX

The warden of New College was a tall, older man dressed impeccably in a blue suit and tie. He looked like he had just conducted a boardroom meeting – he wasn't the traditional academic Nikki had expected. Gareth Flint was bald, with deep lines in his face, and a pair of alarmed but inquisitive grey eyes. They were seated in his office on the first floor, overlooking the pristine lawns of the quadrangle.

"Are you sure she's a student at this college?" he asked as soon as Nikki had finished giving him the details. "I mean, she could be the girlfriend or friend of someone in this college."

"That's what we need to find out without delay. Do you object to her photo being shown to the students? We can do so while interviewing them."

He narrowed his eyes. "I'm afraid that wouldn't be wise. We need to maintain confidentiality. We have a press liaison office at the college, and also at the university. We must not make this news public with consulting them first." Mr Flint's no-nonsense attitude had just become even sharper.

You mean you have a reputation to keep, Nikki thought to

herself in silence. Aloud she said, "Then how do you suggest we get a positive ID?"

Monty stirred beside her. "Can we get access to the student ID database? That should have photos of the current students. We can use our facial recognition software to match her image."

Nikki looked at him gratefully. He blinked at her once. Mr Flint nodded. "I think that would be appropriate, yes." He looked at the open screen of his laptop. "I can give you log-ins for our database. Again, these log-ins are strictly confidential."

Nikki nodded. "Thank you. But we do need to interview some students. If the victim is a student here, we need to know who her friends were." She held Mr Flint's eyes, aware he didn't like her suggestion, or her tone.

"Without doing that, we cannot solve the case. It will be done with total confidentiality," Nikki added. "I very much doubt the students questioned would speak to their friends about it, after we warn them of the consequences. We know how to handle these situations."

Mr Flint appeared to assess Nikki's words carefully. "Very well. In any case, I need to give them an explanation as to why they cannot go outside today. An incident is all I will disclose for now, while you conduct your investigation."

"The key task is to keep the media from learning about this," Nikki said. "Please warn the press office, and tell them to alert you immediately in the case of any journalist making enquiries. We are on your side with regards to keeping this from the media."

Mr Flint looked more pleased now. His shoulders dropped a touch, and the formal tone in his voice faded.

"I have alerted them already, but will pass on your specific message." He looked a little lost all of a sudden. "I've never heard of this happening in New College. I've been the warden for the last five years, but I was an undergraduate student here in the late seventies."

Nikki calculated swiftly, putting Mr Flint in his mid-sixties. He looked good for his age.

He sighed. "I've been in touch with the college fellows and trustees. They will keep their silence, don't worry. Let me get your log-ins."

Once they received the credentials, Nikki and Monty went outside. The quadrangle was beautiful, the emerald-green central lawn enclosed by the turrets and towers of the stone building. It was deserted today, and Nikki knew that was unusual. Faces peered down from the windows above. The students would be texting their friends, and word would spread sooner than later.

As they approached the white forensic tent, Nikki couldn't help thinking how alien the stark, clinical tent looked against the centuries-old college rampart walls, and the green ivy cascading down its length. The white-coated SOC officers, the police in their high visibility jackets – all of it seemed disjointed, not belonging in this quiet place of study.

When Nikki entered the tent again, Dr Sheila Raman was crouching by the body and didn't look back. Moving forward, she examined the head, then sighed. Nikki moved to the other side of the victim's body and the pathologist looked up at her. Sorrow clouded her features, softening her normally sharp eyes.

"So young," she whispered sadly. "Do you have an ID?"

"Not yet, Sheila," Nikki said. "But we're looking. I'm hoping her necklace and earring can help – the students might recognise that on her. Her face is well preserved, which means there's a hope of getting a match on the facial recognition software. Her clothes are that of a student, I think."

Dr Raman looked down at the woman. "Yes, I'd say so. A young woman's attire." She opened up her briefcase and put down a sterile sheet, then lay out her instruments.

She looked up at Nikki. "Please help me take the rectal temperature."

Nikki moved the victim's shoulders and waist to the left, lifting the body up and taking care to touch as little as she could, even with her gloved hands. Sheila undid the jeans, and inserted the rectal probe. Once Sheila was satisfied with the reading, they laid the body down gently, to its original position.

Henrietta "Hetty" Barfield, the bubbly and normally cheerful head of the SOC came into the tent. Her good mood was absent today as she stared at the victim, and murmured hello to Nikki and Sheila.

"What's the ambient temperature?" Sheila asked Hetty.

"About eighteen degrees, but I take it you want last night's as well. It would've been in a range of ten to fifteen degrees."

Sheila concentrated, her forehead creasing. "The victim is thin, which means her body would have lost heat quickly. Given the difference between rectal and ambient temperature, I would say death is no more than seven hours. Which means around two a.m."

"Does she have rigor mortis in the large muscles?" Nikki asked.

Sheila gave Nikki one of her rare smiles. "Good observation. Yes, it's starting in the large muscles but not widespread as yet. Rigor mortis only starts in the large muscles between six to twelve hours after death. So death couldn't have been six hours ago."

Sheila examined the victim's head and neck, then ran her gloved hands down the back. Hetty and Nikki helped her to observe the chest by lifting the victim partially again. Nikki was suddenly thankful the note from the girl's coat was now in Monty's pocket.

Sheila stood and watched the body, frowning again. "From what I've seen so far, the head injury and massive blood loss following rupture of intra-abdominal organs is the main cause of death. Unless of course, that head injury occurred prior to her being here."

"What do you think? Was she killed before she arrived here?" Nikki asked.

"Given where the rock is, right against her head, I doubt that. She hit that rock hard enough for her skull to splinter. Either she was hit with it, or she fell. Is that your working assumption – that she fell from the ramparts?"

"Yes." Nikki nodded. "I doubt she was hit with the rock outside the college, then brought here. It would attract attention, even if she was brought through one of the back routes." She paused to think, her mind sneaking around strange corners. The body could've been hidden, then placed here, to fool her into thinking the woman fell from the ramparts. She dismissed the idea. The body was too fresh for it to have been hidden for any length of time.

Sheila lifted up the right hand.

"No nicotine stains under the fingernails. But there are signs of trauma in the hands. The nails are damaged, some ripped off. She might have tried to hold onto the wall as she fell. And there's small lacerations in the knuckles."

Nikki added, "And no marks on her neck to show she was strangled. I can't see any obvious bruises on the head. I don't think she got into a fight."

"No. If she fell from the ramparts, either she was pushed, or she fell."

Hetty was crouched by the head. Her face was flushed from kneeling close to the victim's neck. She stood up, lowered her mask and blew a strand of black hair from her face. With a sterile swab stick, she had lifted the necklace and had a close look at it.

"That's an expensive chain. Twenty-four carat gold unless I'm mistaken. My dad used to run a jewellery shop."

"Her clothes aren't cheap either," Nikki said. "I looked at the label of her jeans."

Hetty smiled. "Not many of us commoners study in Oxford, eh?"

"That has changed," Sheila said. "One of my friends is a Merton college tutor. She said about a third of their first-year intake now comes from state schools."

"But two thirds don't," Hetty replied, "and that's the point."

The tent flap behind them lifted and Monty poked his head in. He offered them a tight smile, then his eyes focused on Nikki.

"Can I have a word please?"

SEVEN

"Just got a call back from Kristy," Monty said. "Facial recognition can do wonders, it seems. The photo we took matches an image on the student database."

Nikki looked up at Monty expectantly. Monty held her eyes as he spoke. "A third-year student called Chloe Pierson. She studied history at New College." Monty handed Nikki his phone.

On the screen, she saw the bright, smiling face of a young woman, her brown hair cascading to her shoulders. Her grey eyes had a hint of mischief, and the smile on her face seemed to suggest she was laughing at a joke she'd just heard. Nikki's heart constricted as she gazed at the open, happy face of the young woman, the eyes full of hope. That light was now gone, and her family would be plunged into darkness too when they learned the terrible news.

Nikki closed her eyes and sighed. Then she scrolled down the screen, noting Chloe's phone number and the college address

"We didn't find a phone, or purse," Nikki said. Her jaws flexed as anger tightened her chest. Someone had done this to

Chloe. Granted, no one could tell anything from a photo, but Nikki had a sixth sense Chloe didn't have mental health issues severe enough to take her own life. Those open eyes, that frank smile, and the happy expression on her face didn't belong to someone who was faking it. If anything, Chloe seemed like a person willing to take on the world – and dabble in some risks while she was at it.

Nikki cautioned herself against assuming too much. She hated the loss of a young life, and at the back of her soul loomed the ever-present shadow of the loss of her brother, Tommy. The brother she never got to know but would miss forever. She was getting emotional, and that wouldn't do. She had a job to complete.

When she looked up at Monty, she saw a mellowness in his eyes. As if he understood without her speaking a word. He reached for his phone, and she handed it back to him. She realised she had been clutching it tightly, and she relaxed as she their fingers touched, his skin warm against hers, for a brief second. Her heart jolted as Monty held her eyes, a slight smile hovering on his lips.

"Mr Flint is getting in touch with the parents. They should be here soon." A tightness in his lips replaced the smile. Like Nikki, he knew the grim task now facing the parents.

Nikki nodded. Monty continued, "I also think stopping all students getting out of the college will be a problem. It's only going to fuel the rumour mill, and you never know, we might even see students climbing on the rampart."

Nikki considered that. "But that's worse than students walking around to see the crime scene, no? I'll have a partition put up to shield the view."

"Exactly. We're lucky this happened down the side, and not in front of the main entrance."

"Okay..." Nikki sighed. "I guess that makes sense. You're right, we can't stop the students from going about their day. It was more of a concern when we didn't have the ID." Nikki was silent for a few seconds. "But the killer might still be here. We need to start interviewing some students."

"I've asked Mr Flint already. He's reaching out to Chloe's subject tutors to find out who studied with her. He's also sent a couple of the college fellows to Chloe's corridor. I told him they can ask around for her friends, but not to enter her room. The porters have the keys. Shall we have a look?"

Back in the quadrangle, the former hush was now punctured by voices and the patter of feet. Students were up and about, perhaps heading up from their breakfast, and getting ready for the day's tutorials. Although none of the uniforms had stepped inside the quadrangle, Nikki wondered if some of the students knew already. News of police presence, and a white forensic tent, would spread like wildfire.

Monty looked around him, stuffing his big hands inside his coat pockets.

"Do third-year students live on college premises? Don't they move out after the first year?"

"Actually," Nikki said, "they move out in the second year, but for the final year a lot of them move back in. It's meant to be easier to meet with the college tutors who live on site. It's a bit of an Oxford tradition."

"How do you know? You studied somewhere up north, right?"

"Durham, yes. But I had friends who worked in the Oxford colleges. As a teenager I also worked as a library assistant at the Bodleian."

"Did you now?" Monty raised his eyebrows. "Kept that one quiet."

Nikki tapped the side of her nose. "Dark horse, me."

"So, any more nuggets of wisdom about the colleges?"

Nikki shrugged. "What I do know is that although Oxford town has changed, the colleges operate in the same way. We found that out last year…"

Monty nodded, the mirth fading from his lips. "Another student. I hope this isn't a pattern."

It had been a year since they had investigated the death of a student at a large party. It had been a difficult case to crack, and Nikki had suffered during the investigation.

"Me too," she said shortly.

"Come on then, let's find justice for Chloe."

The pair approached the main doors of the quad, where the porter with his belt of keys and the warden were waiting for them. Mr Flint's eyes slid from Nikki to Dooley. "You wanted to look at Chloe's room?"

"Yes," Nikki said. "And the room will now be a crime scene. Please make sure no one enters."

Mr Flint didn't look happy about it, but he nodded. "I've spoken to the Piersons. They will be here shortly. I'll let you know when they arrive."

"Thanks."

Nikki followed Dooley as he went up the narrow, spiral staircase that was made of smooth, ancient stones. It felt cool here, even with the summer sun starting to build heat outside.

They climbed to the third floor and walked down the yellow-grey stone-flanked corridor. Dooley opened a door and, just before they entered, a head poked out of the door opposite. The woman, with frizzy blonde hair, quickly pulled back again, only showing her eyes through the only slightly ajar door. She'd be their first interview. But for now, their priority was searching Chloe's room and seeing what they could find out about who Chloe was.

. . .

Chloe's room was a typical student dig, with a poster of a male rock star on the wall, bare chested and pouting. There was a single bed, a built-in wardrobe on the wall opposite and, next to it, a small sink and mirror recessed in the wall. Above a desk, timetables were stuck on a corkboard and a bookshelf was filled with textbooks. A laptop and papers were scattered on the desk, and a printer sat beneath it, cables snaking their way behind.

Nikki didn't see anything unusual at first sight. They said goodbye to Dooley and put on gloves. Monty lifted the sheet over the bed gingerly, then the duvet. The bed was slept in, possibly by more than one person. Under Nikki's instructions, Monty lifted the duvet more. The sheets were creased and had some stains. Scene of Crime would up here soon, and taking samples. Nikki pulled out her phone and left a message for Hetty, giving her the room number.

She went to the window and looked out. The room faced the rear grounds, which were extensive. Landscaped gardens, dotted with mature trees, rolled down to the rear ramparts. From here, the staff quarters were visible, and farther out, to the left, behind the ramparts, the large structure of Magdalene College by the banks of the river Cherwell.

Beyond the staff quarters, the rampart walls encircled the college like a wraith. A bank of trees hid the rampart walls in places, and through the foliage, Nikki caught glimpses of cars on the High Street.

On an impulse, she checked the windowsill and ledges. No footprints – not that she expected to see any. Chloe had stood on the rampart walls at around two in the morning. Young people did stupid things, and Nikki felt Chloe had either been drunk, high on drugs, or someone had pushed her.

Behind her, Monty was looking under the bed. He went to the desk, and put the laptop to one side, then started to go through the papers. Nikki noticed a couple of photos in frames on the bookshelf above the desk. Three smiling young women stood in skiing outfits against a white mountain slope. With a gloved hand, Nikki examined it. The woman in the middle looked like Chloe. The others were similar in age to her. Nikki took a photo of it with her phone. The next photo was taken in the summer, in a park. Again, Chloe was recognisable in the middle, flanked by an elderly couple, clearly her parents. Chloe was gripping the man's elbow, and leaning towards him, laughing. It was a happy, sunny picture, a bygone summer's memories held in a frame. Nikki's heart lurched in pain when she thought of Chloe's parents. She wasn't looking forward to speaking to them.

The last and much smaller photo frame was interesting. It was circular, a round silver frame that looked old. It held the faded colour photo of a woman. Nikki examined her face closely. She was young, less than thirty, or perhaps early thirties at the most. Her hair was blonde, and her eyes, the shape of her face, held a resemblance to Chloe as a young woman. Nikki glanced back at the family photo. Was the older woman in that photo the same person in the smaller frame? Nikki's eyes moved from one to the other, but she couldn't make her mind up.

"Found a suitcase with some clothes and books inside. The case was open," Monty said, before peering at the photos. "Is that her grandmother? Or maybe an aunt?" he suggested, indicating the small frame.

"I don't know..." Nikki pursed her lips together. "It might be her gran, or nan. Doesn't look much like a younger version of her mother, does it?"

Monty shook his head slowly. "Nope."

Nikki took more photos, and then crouched by the suitcase on the floor. It held a mixture of clothes that perhaps Chloe didn't wear anymore. Old pyjamas, gym tops and underwear. Nikki looked in the pockets of the suitcase and found nothing. Monty held up a couple of notebooks he'd placed on the bed.

"I found these inside. She's written poems and kept a journal." He handed them to Nikki, and she looked through them briefly. They held verses, with some pictures drawn alongside them, abstract forms sketched with a pen and pencil. Nikki didn't have time to read the poems, but she would look at them later. Monty put the notebooks in evidence bags, along with some of the clothes.

Nikki's phone rang. It was Mr Flint. "The parents are here, if you want to see them."

"That was quick," Nikki said.

"They live in Abingdon and were at a garden centre near Oxford today. They're at the student liaison office, which is downstairs, across the corridor from my room."

"We'll be there in two minutes."

Nikki informed Monty, and they left.

EIGHT

The elderly couple sitting on the brown Chesterfield sofa looked haggard, their faces lined with worry. Both of them stood up as Nikki and Monty entered. The woman spoke first. She was small and prim, dressed in a green vest and jeans with black shoes. Her lips quivered as she spoke.

"Is this true? What's happened to our Chloe?"

"Please have a seat," Nikki said, and the couple obeyed.

The student liaison office was spacious, with a brown desk and chairs arranged around it. Indoor plants were arranged on both sides of the desk. Nikki showed them her warrant card, as Monty shut the door. She introduced herself and Monty.

"Yes, unfortunately Chloe Pierson was found dead this morning by the rampart walls of the college. Her death might be an accident, but we are keeping all our options open."

The woman's face turned from white to grey, and it looked like she might vomit. The man's chest stopped moving as if he couldn't breathe anymore. His grey eyes were hollowed out with grief, and he couldn't speak.

"Can you please confirm your names?" Nikki asked, looking

at the woman first. The elderly lady took out a tissue and wiped her eyes and the red tip of her nose.

"I'm Angela, Chloe's stepmother. And this is Jeffrey, her dad."

The man stared at Nikki and inclined his head once.

"Excuse me, but is Chloe's mother not available?" Nikki felt silly asking the question.

"No, she died many years ago, when Chloe was young." Angela looked at Jeffrey, who still looked like a ghost. Colour had drained from his face entirely, and he seemed incapable of speech. Nikki was concerned.

"Mr Pierson, are you alright?"

With an effort, Jeffrey opened his mouth. It seemed like invisible fingers pulled at his lips, forcing him to speak.

"Yes." He cleared his throat. He subsided into silence again. Nikki recognised the signs of shock in the hollowness of his eyes, and the slump in his spine. He sagged on the sofa, refusing to make eye contact.

Nikki thought back to the photos she had seen in Chloe's room. The woman in that small round frame. Her blonde hair, and sad smile, all faded. Was that Chloe's mother? She took out her phone, and showed the photo to Jeffrey and Angela.

"Yes," Jeffrey nodded. "That's Connie – Constance – Chloe's mother. Chloe didn't remember her much, but she wanted to, obviously. She kept that photo as a memento."

Jeffrey lapsed into silence, his head bowed again.

"Mr Pierson..." DI Monty Sen leaned forward, clasping his hands in front of his knees. "I know this is extremely difficult for you. But we need to find out what happened to Chloe. And you can help us more than anyone else, perhaps. You want to know, don't you?"

A flicker of emotion appeared in Jeffrey's lifeless eyes. His gaunt, white cheeks shook, and then he spoke.

"Yes. Yes, of course I do."

"Can you start by telling us what happened to Chloe's mother?"

Jeffrey shut his eyes, as if trying to remember.

"She... she left one day and never came back. Never heard from her again. I did search for her, and got the police involved, but they never found her."

Monty turned his head to look at Nikki, who was frowning. "You mean Chloe's mother went missing?"

"Yes, she did, unfortunately. This was a long time ago." Jeffrey's face started crumbling, and it was like watching a chainsaw running through a painting. His jaws clamped together, and his nostrils flared as he tried to control his emotions and failed. Angela reached over and put her hand over his.

"How old was Chloe when her mother went missing?"

"She was three. I told her about her mother all her life. Angela looked after Chloe as well, and for that I am grateful." Jeffrey face contorted in a rictus of grief, and Angela tightened her grip on his hand.

Jeffrey's voice was hollow, almost echoing in the room's silence. "I shall never forget. Before Connie left us, she used to tell me to look after Chloe if something happened to her. I couldn't do that." He closed his eyes.

"Why did she say that?"

Jeffrey raised his head slowly to look at Nikki through the veil of heavy sadness. "Connie suffered with depression. She had tried to kill herself once, by taking an overdose. I found her on time and saved her. She was better on medication after that."

"Until she disappeared? Was it blamed on her mental health?"

"Yes. Eventually, anyway, when the police, or anyone, couldn't find her."

Monty spoke. "And what did you think happened?"

Jeffrey shook his head. "I don't know. I can't think of that right now."

Nikki touched Monty's arm, and he nodded. There was no point in discussing Chloe's mother until the Piersons were in the right frame of mind.

"Connie left me, and now so has Chloe."

Jeffrey's last word dissolved in a sob, and he succumbed to his grief, his head lowering over his chest. His body shuddered, and Angela put a hand on his shoulder, comforting him.

Nikki had seen this time and again, and the emotion never failed to touch her. She, too, had lost a brother once. In some dark, hidden corner of her soul, she felt the sharp stab of everlasting regret. The poison dripped again, slowly filling the wound that had never healed.

She sat back, giving the couple some time to themselves. Monty stepped out of the room and reappeared with water in a plastic cup. He offered it to Mr Pierson, who accepted it with thanks.

Nikki gave them some time and had a whispered discussion with Monty. He was on his phone already, looking for reports of a missing person.

Nikki asked, "When did you last see Chloe?" She addressed the question to both of them.

Angela answered first. "She came home for the Easter break in April. She was with us for a week, then she met up with her boyfriend."

"What's his name?"

"Mark Ofori. He came to our house once." Angela lapsed into silence. Her expression had changed, and she seemed unwilling to talk any more. Her eyes flickered to her husband, who also remained quiet.

"What did you think about Mark?" Nikki asked the obvious question. She suspected there wasn't much about Mark that endeared him to the couple.

"He was a young lad whom Chloe liked," Angela said, her manner still evasive.

Nikki decided to state the obvious. "You didn't like him?"

"It wasn't that. He was just quiet, and kept to himself. A little surly if you like."

There was silence for a few seconds. Nikki thought this might be an important moment. Most murder victims knew their killers. Mark was definitely a suspect.

"It's critical that we find out more about Mark. Can you please tell us what you thought of him?"

Jeffrey sighed. "He didn't like some paintings I got from my ancestors. One of them showed King Leopold of Belgium posing with African kings. The kings were bowing in front of him. There was a couple of them, another showed Cecil Rhodes in Africa. I never thought anything of them. They were just old paintings on the wall. But I can see how it can be offensive to Mark, who's African himself, obviously."

Monty enquired, "He's not British?"

Jeffrey looked perplexed, then cleared his throat, an embarrassed look on his face. "Yes, that's what I meant. He's of African descent, but he was born and raised in England."

"Was there anything else that might have meant you didn't get on with him?" Nikki tried.

"Not really," Jeffrey said. "He was a quiet lad. I mean, the pictures offended him, and he told me. We all know what happened in Africa in those days. I felt a little ashamed to be honest. My great grandfather was a surveyor for a coal miner's company. He was often posted in Africa. That's where the paintings came from. I took the paintings down, and that was that as far as I was concerned."

"Did you speak to him after?"

"Yes, we talked, but not much. He came from a simple family. His father was a bus driver. He's an intelligent lad who did well for himself." Jeffrey shrugged. "He's different from us, obviously. But then again, all young people are."

Nikki glanced at Angela, who had a stony look on her face. "What about you, Mrs Pierson? What did you think of Mark?"

Angela shrugged. "I didn't interact with him much, to be honest. Not really sure what you want me to say."

Interesting. Nikki wondered if Angela was keeping her thoughts to herself.

"How did Mark behave with Chloe? Did their relationship seem normal?"

Angela said, "As far as I could see, yes, it was. They went for walks together. They also stayed in their room a lot."

Nikki decided to leave it for now, but she wanted to meet Mark as soon as she could.

"How was Chloe when you saw her?" she asked both of them.

Angela answered first. "Fine, as far as I could tell. She seemed happy, like her usual self." She turned to her husband, who nodded.

"Yes, I think so. I picked up her and Mark from the train station. It was nice to have her back." He smiled, and then misery overcast his features like cloud coming over the sun.

"When they left, did they come back to Oxford?"

"No. There was a music festival or something in the Cotswolds, near Cirencester. They left on Friday to spend the weekend there."

"Did you know the name of the festival?"

"No, sorry."

"Mr Pierson, I know this is hard for you. And you, Angela. But can you think of anyone who might want to harm Chloe? Or anyone that Chloe had trouble with?"

The couple looked at each other, then shook their heads.

"I can't think of anyone, or any incident like that," Jeffrey murmured, and his wife agreed.

Nikki looked down at her hands briefly. She had to ask the difficult questions now. She had no choice.

"As far as you are aware, did Chloe take recreational drugs?"

Jeffrey and Angela stared at Nikki.

"I'm sorry to ask this, but we need to know. I'm referring to street drugs like ecstasy, cocaine, amphetamine or speed and so on."

Jeffrey raised his eyebrows, and Angela shrugged, bending her lips in an expression of denial.

"Well, I know that she smoked," Jeffrey said. "I tried to talk her out of it, as I smoked when I was younger. But apart from that, I don't know."

"Actually, come to think of it," Angela said, "I'm pretty sure I smelt cannabis on Mark's clothes. After they came back from a walk. I'm certain it was that."

"On Mark's clothes but not Chloe's?" Nikki asked.

"Well, they were standing close together, so I guess so." Angela waved a hand. For some reason, Nikki didn't like her attitude. There was something about Angela that bothered her, but she couldn't put a finger on it.

Nikki glanced at Monty, to see if he had any more questions. "Mr Pierson," Monty asked, "how did Chloe's mother disappear?"

"She left after dinner one day, to buy something at the local corner shop. She never returned. She was doing well as far as the depression was concerned. She was winning over the disease, so to speak. She had been taking the antidepressants for weeks. When she didn't return, I put little Chloe in a pushchair and went looking for her. I didn't find her. None of the neighbours had seen her. So, I went out in the car with Chloe. No sign of Connie. She didn't return that night." Jeffrey paused to take a breath.

"The next morning, I got the police involved. Over that

week, the search party got bigger. There was no social media in those days. The police spread the news on the papers and radio, TV."

Jeffrey stopped again. "We never found her. It torments me to this day. My heart tells me she committed suicide. As to why we never found her body – I don't know."

"Where did you live then?"

"In Wolvercote, near Oxford."

Nikki frowned. "Oh, right. That's not far from north Oxford." And close to Jericho, where her mother lived, she thought to herself in silence.

Monty looked at Angela. "When did you meet your husband?"

"Chloe was six years old then. I moved in with Jeff a year later. I became her stepmother."

"You didn't have any more children?"

A shadow moved across Angela's face. Nikki saw it. She suspected Angela had wanted more children.

"No," Angela said.

NINE

"What did you think of the Piersons?" Monty asked as they made their way to meet the porter, Chris Dooley.

"Jeffrey's grief is genuine. I thought Angela was a little distant."

"I thought so too. She's not Chloe's mother, though. Her mother is the woman in that photo on her shelf, right?"

"Yes." Nikki considered the photo again. She needed to speak to Jeffrey again – and find out more about Chloe's mother, Constance. "Can you ask one of the lads to check the Missing Persons database? I want Constance Pierson's files."

Monty nodded and called Nish as they reached the third-floor landing, where Dooley was already waiting. He walked ahead of them, down the corridor, and unlocked Chloe's room.

"You carry on here, I'll have a look outside," Nikki said. Monty did a mock salute.

"Aye, aye, captain."

Nikki rolled her eyes, and turned back to the porter, Dooley.

"Mr Dooley—"

"Call me Chris, please." The man smiled nervously.

"Chris, you said you heard voices inside the quad last night. Is that correct?"

"Yes. I was on night duty. I go out for a ciggy, and walk around the front of the rampart, where the cars park inside the college. The quad grounds are closed by a door so no one gets out, but there is a small gate with a fob key. I have one, and so do the students and staff. But I didn't see anyone come out."

"What sort of voices did you hear? Could you make out what they were saying?"

Chris scratched his neck. "No. I heard some shouts. It sounded like someone calling out to another person. I couldn't make out the names. I could hear running feet. I did walk down the left of the rampart, to be honest." Chris stared at Nikki, sudden fear appearing in his face. "Sorry I didn't tell you that before. But I wanted to check."

"No problem," Nikki assured him. "Carry on."

"I went down the path where... where..."

"We found the body. The crime scene."

"Yes." Chris seemed relieved Nikki said the words. "And I didn't see anything. I did look up at the ramparts. I didn't hear any sounds, nor did I see anyone up there."

"Did you have a torch?"

Chris looked a little embarrassed. "Uh... yes, I did, but I left it at the office, in the porters' lodge. I mean, I thought it was a couple of drunk students, that's all. I hear them occasionally. Sometimes they come back from nightclubs and act silly. Not for long though, all the students, no matter how drunk, know they can't make a mess in the quad." Chris stopped and frowned, looking away from Nikki.

"What is it?" she asked.

"Actually, at night the quad is protected with a gate. The fob keys we have allow access to the halls. Where the students live, I mean. But the students can't get into the quad at night. So this would've been outside it. Between the quad and the rampart walls." Chris shook his head. "It must've been some students coming back from a night out."

"But you didn't see anyone. It was night, so the voices carried in the silence, correct?"

Chris nodded. He looked shamefaced. "Sorry, I should've told you that before. Anyway, I walked past the uh... crime scene, but there was nothing there that got my attention."

"What time was this?"

"Around one a.m. I remember I walked around the perimeter and got back to the office and I checked the time."

"And you saw no one in the perimeter?"

Chris shook his head. "No, sorry."

"So the voices you heard were outside the quad because the entrance to the quad is shut at night. Do you have keys?

"Yes, us and security. The police spoke to them as well. The guards didn't hear or see anything."

Nikki thought for a while. Chris could be mistaken and there was a chance the voices did indeed come from inside the quad. Maybe a fellow or lecturer had keys to get into the quad, and they let some students in. Nikki was well aware of the Oxford drinking clubs and secret societies, where many of the academic staff played a low-key leadership role.

"We will speak to the security guards again," Nikki said. Chris nodded, looking uneasy at being questioned. Nikki didn't think he was being cagey. He seemed to be speaking the truth. But genuine liars were hard to spot – they hid it well.

The door opposite opened a crack again, drawing Nikki's attention. Through the sliver of the opening, she could see the blonde curls of hair. The door closed but remained open a fraction, as if the person inside wanted to hear what they were saying.

As Nikki approached, the door instantly shut. Nikki knocked, then put her ear to the wood. A soft gasp and the sound of rapidly retreating steps came from the other side. Nikki pushed, but it was locked.

"Hello? May I come in?"

There was silence for a while. Then steps came closer to the door, and a woman's voice cleared her throat. "Who're you?"

"If you open the door, I can tell you." Nikki didn't want to shout out her name and title on the corridor.

Another silence, then the door opened. The worried face of a young woman appeared. Her blonde hair had dark roots, and it was straggly, falling over her face. Nikki showed her warrant card. The woman's eyes got wider, and her mouth opened.

"If you let me in," Nikki said gently, "we can talk."

The woman shut her mouth with an effort and opened the door wider. Nikki walked into a room that was a carbon copy of Chloe's room. The walls here had a lot more posters, mostly prints of modern art, and political slogans of the Communist Party of Britain.

The woman was dressed in yellow slacks, and she had a baggy blue top on. Her blue eyes blinked as she stared at Nikki.

"What's your name?"

"Jemima. Dixon." She added her last name slowly. "What's going on? You're the police, right? A detective." Her smooth forehead frowned as she said the last word.

"Yes. I'm Detective Inspector Nikki Gill of Thames Valley Police."

"Why were you in Chloe's room?" Jemima blurted out, her chest heaving. "What's happened?"

"Why don't we sit down?" Nikki indicated the chairs, but Jemima sat on the bed. Nikki grabbed a chair.

"Do you know Chloe?" Nikki was careful to use the present tense.

"Yes. I study English Lit, and we had some common tutorials in history of languages. She did History." Jemima blinked a few times and her impatience surfaced again. "Why were you in her room? Isn't she inside?"

"Are you good friends with Chloe?"

Jemima's large eyes were frightened. She was pretty, with a longish face, framed well by a long nose and wide mouth. Her eyes dominated her features, and they were restless.

"I am, yes. We hung out together after tutorials. And we live together, as you can see."

"When did you last see Chloe?"

"Last night. I went out, but she stayed in because she had to work on an essay." The frown on Jemima's face got deeper. "Why are you asking?"

Nikki wondered how much to tell her. It depended on how well Jemima knew Chloe.

"I'll tell you in a minute. I have a couple more questions. Does Chloe have a boyfriend?"

"Yes. His name's Mark. He doesn't live here though – he does law at Balliol. He's in a house in Summertown with his friends."

"Does Chloe have any other friends here apart from you?"

"A couple, yes. She has other friends who live elsewhere."

"Do you know how I can contact them, please? I need their names, addresses and phone numbers."

"I can have a look." Jemima sighed, her cheeks now losing colour. She looked like she was going to be sick. "Oh my god... What... what's happened?" she whispered.

Nikki couldn't let the rumour mill go into a frenzy, nor could she tell Jemima everything. But Jemima needed to know the basic truth. Only then would she be completely cooperative. She leaned forward, and lowered her voice in sympathy.

"I'm so sorry Jemima, Chloe's dead."

Jemima seemed to shrink inside her body, her chest caving in. Her cheeks turned white. She couldn't speak, although her mouth opened.

"What?" she finally whispered.

"I'm sorry," Nikki repeated. "I know this is a shock for you."

"But... I saw her last night. We came home from tutorial, and she went up to her room. Right here. Then I went out."

Nikki was scribbling in her notebook. "What time was that?"

"About six p.m."

"Did you see her before you left the building? Did you knock on her door, or see her anywhere else?"

"No. I left to meet up with my friends in town."

"Where was your tutorial?"

"At All Souls College. That's where our tutor's office is. His name's Jonathan Saul. He's a professor of history there."

"Was Mr Saul Chloe's main tutor?"

Jemima hesitated before nodding. Nikki took the details of Chloe's boyfriend, Mark, and the two girls that Jemima knew who were friends with Chloe.

"Fiona and Sally – do they live here?"

"Sally does, on the third floor. We're all final-year history students at New College. Fiona's at Merton College, and she lives out, in Cowley."

"Did Chloe belong to any societies?"

Jemima took a breath and held it for a second before letting go. "Yes." She raised a hand. "Wait. I can't believe this is happening." Her eyes were red already, and now she wiped tears. "Is this really true? Chloe's dead? But how?"

"I can't tell you that right now, but unfortunately, yes, she is dead. This is now a police investigation, and any help you can give us is very valuable. Now, can you tell me which societies Chloe belonged to?"

Jemima hung her head, then gripped her forehead. She brushed hair from her face, and looked at the brown carpet.

"Please tell me what happened." Jemima looked up at her. Her cheeks were stained with tears. "How did she die?"

Nikki pressed her lips together. "Was Chloe your best friend?"

"We were besties, yes."

"She didn't suffer," Nikki said gently. "From what we can see, it was a quick death. I will speak to you again, but that's all I can tell you for now."

Jemima covered her mouth. Her eyes snapped shut. Nikki gave her a few seconds to herself.

Then she asked Jemima again about the societies, as she knew a lot of the Oxonians' social lives revolved around them. Jemima appeared to think carefully before she answered.

"We were both members of a drinking club, but these groups are more active in the first and second years. We have to focus on our studies now. That's what we did. We still had the annual ball of the Beaverton Society this summer. It's held every year in July." Jemima sighed and sorrow creased her face. "I guess she won't be attending that now."

"I need the details of who to contact in the Beaverton Society and the drinking club. What was the club called?"

"TITS – Tequila Imbibing Total Sluts. It's a New College institution." Jemima smiled sadly. "We have members from every college, but it started here."

"Sounds like fun." Nikki smiled back, feeling Jemima's grief weigh down the air in the room. There was genuine sorrow in Jemima's face – that broken, lost look in her eyes that meant she felt helpless. Nikki sat down next to her and touched her hand.

"We will find out exactly what happened to Chloe, okay? We will get answers. I can promise you that."

Jemima looked at Nikki with hollow eyes, as if Nikki spoke in a language she didn't understand.

"Do you have friends you can talk to? You can tell them, it's okay."

Jemima nodded.

"Call them now," Nikki said. "If you want to speak to me, I

will be in Chloe's room." She paused, removing her hand from Jemima's, but squeezing her shoulder once.

"Was Chloe bothered by anything recently? Did she seem worried, or anxious?"

Nikki felt a slight stiffening in Jemima's stance. The young woman tucked a loose strand of hair behind her ear. She stared at the floor, not making eye contact with Nikki.

"Not that I noticed, no." Jemima shrugged once. She looked askance at Nikki, then averted her eyes. For the first time, Nikki didn't believe her.

"Are you sure?"

Jemima sighed. "Well, she was worried about her work. The prof wasn't happy with the way her degree thesis was going. She had used AI to write part of it, and he told her she couldn't do that. She was stressed about it, as she had to rewrite almost five thousand words."

"Is that all? She wasn't worried about anything else?"

"Not as far as I know." Jemima looked at Nikki fully now, but Nikki still wondered if she was speaking the truth.

"If you think of anything else, please let us know."

"Where did you go?" Monty asked. He was on his knees in Chloe's room, his hands on a printer he had pulled out from under the desk.

"Luckily, Chloe's best friend lives in the room opposite." Nikki told Monty about her meeting with Jemima. "Hopefully we can speak to Fiona and Sally today."

Monty stood, grimacing as his knees clicked. "I couldn't open the laptop as it's password protected," he said. "And there's no sign of a phone..."

"No phone on the body, either. But she had one, we know that from Jemima. She's given us Chloe's number. We can get the call list, even if we don't have the actual phone."

"I did find this behind the bed though." Monty showed Nikki a matchbox. The word *Cargo* was inscribed on the box.

"I looked it up," Monty said. "It's a nightclub in the outskirts of Oxford. Looks big, with loads of DJs. I've heard of it, actually. Not just students go to it – some of my party animal friends too." Monty grinned.

"Didn't know you had friends like that."

"It's not really my thing, and I don't have time anyway. But chances are our victim went there. Ergo, she could've been a party animal as well."

"Maybe," Nikki said, realising she had forgotten to ask Jemima if Chloe was a hardcore clubber. She might've been, Nikki realised, given her love of drinking.

Monty had taken off the duvet and revealed the bedsheets again. "Two people slept here, definitely. I've taken some swabs, but it might be optimistic. Hetty will have a better idea."

He strolled over to the sink and mirror, and Nikki joined him. There was a makeup bag, and a few shades of lipstick and gloss were on the shelf below the mirror.

"Bag those for DNA samples," Nikki said.

"I've already taken one, and the electric toothbrush," Monty replied, raising his eyebrows.

Nikki grinned at the hurt expression on his face. "I knew you would. Just testing."

"It's me who was charged with observing you, remember?"

"That was a while ago, Inspector Sen, unless you've forgotten?"

"Oh, I'm still watching..." His brown chestnut eyes danced with light, and Nikki felt a knot loosen deep in her belly.

She blinked and looked away, embarrassed and aroused at the same time.

"I'm sorry," Monty said. Nikki paused, closing her eyes. She didn't mind, but she didn't want Monty to know that.

"It's okay," she replied lightly. She glanced at him and

smiled. He had a serious expression – she much preferred the light-hearted banter. "As long as you watch and learn."

The smile returned on Monty's lips. "If you insist."

They resumed their search of the room, each covering the areas the other had previously checked. Using her phone torch, Nikki scanned carefully under the bed. Suddenly, something at the skirting board caught her eye. A tuft of carpet rising up, like it had come loose from the underlay and floorboards. The suitcase must have hidden it before.

"Monty, I think there's something here..."

She shuffled backwards and up and, gripping the foot of the bed, moved it to one side. Now it was clear where the carpet was raised. Nikki's and Monty's eyes met, both of them aware of the significance.

With a gloved hand, Monty gripped the edge of the carpet and pulled. It came off easily and revealed that the underlay had been cut out, and there was a hole in the floorboards. Nikki shone her torch, the beam of the light picking up a darkly metallic object.

"Bingo," Monty whispered.

TEN

Monty pulled out the object, which was a flat, rectangular box with a lid and a simple latch key. He brushed away the dust, placing it on the carpet.

"Step back," he told Nikki. She looked at him, puzzled.

"This is Oxford, Monty. We're in college accommodation. This thing's not going to blow up in my face – is it?"

"No, but it might contain fungal spores, or gas, or aerosol poison."

Nikki gaped at him. "Aren't you being a bit melodramatic?"

"In this day and age it's best to be careful. Remember the postal workers in America who opened the packets full of anthrax spores?"

Nikki shook her head. "I never knew you were the paranoid type." She suppressed a smile. "Are you scared?" She couldn't imagine the six-foot-four-inches Monty would be frightened about something like this.

Monty rolled his eyes. "I don't care about me, but I'm worried about you. Now, step back please." He shielded the box with his body so she couldn't see, effectively pushing her back.

Nikki swore, and Monty pretended he didn't hear it.

Blocking her vision with his broad back, he opened the box, and stared at the contents.

"No anthrax spores, I take it? No smoke that's making you see double?" Nikki said, peering over his side.

Two phones in a plastic packet. And, next to it, two packets filled with pills. Monty picked a packet of pills.

"I thought ecstasy Dove pills were from my time," he murmured.

"Went clubbing, did you?" Nikki asked immediately. "Dropped pills and stayed up all night?"

Monty grimaced. "I asked for that one, didn't I?" With a knowing smile, he turned his attention back to the box. Next to the pills, there was a tightly wrapped black cellophane packet that took up the rest of the box. Monty took the packet out slowly, hefting it in his hands.

"Might be C4 explosives," Nikki said. "Be careful."

He angled his eyes to her cheeky grin.

"What?" she asked, feigning surprise. "You wanted to be cautious, not me."

Muttering under his breath, Monty put the cellophane packet on the bed. He took the Swiss Army knife on his keyring and selected a small but sharp blade. Before he stuck the knife in, he pressed on the packet once again. It was hard, but there was a give, like it wasn't completely solid. Neither was it soft like putty.

He pressed the tip of the knife into the packet, hesitated a moment, and then pushed it in. When he withdrew the knife, there was a thin coating of white powder on the tip. Nikki was looking over his shoulder, and her hand touched his arm.

Monty got the knife close to his nose to sniff it, and then tasted it. He made a face. "That's bitter."

"Cocaine?" Nikki ventured. She had been in enough drug busts to know what the narcotic looked like. "How much cocaine in there? Two or three hundred grams?"

"About that." Monty set his jaws together. "I hate to think what an Oxford student is doing with a couple of hundred pills and this much cocaine in her room." He looked around him. "Nothing here seems to suggest she was dealing. I didn't find any weighing scales, wraps and so on."

"No, neither did I. She also had two burner phones. Why would she need that?"

She looked at Monty, and she knew they were thinking along the same lines. Burner phones were used by dealers to stay in touch with their suppliers.

"This adds a new dimension to her death." Nikki frowned. "What if the suppliers wanted their goods back? They could've killed her?"

"No sign of trauma on her body," Monty said. Then he dropped his voice. "And don't forget the note in her pocket." He cocked his head to one side as if a new thought occurred to him. "Have you had any contact with an OCN before? Either here, or in London."

OCN was the common abbreviation for an organised crime network. Nikki frowned, deep in thought. "Not recently, no," she said eventually. "But it might be a possibility. Three years ago the Major Crime Unit finally got the top boys of an Albanian drug-importing gang. I was the SIO. I testified against them, so my name would've come up in the court papers."

"This feels different though, doesn't it? I mean, an Albanian drug smuggler in London and a student here?" Monty raised both hands and shrugged. "But you never know, I guess."

"I guess not," Nikki said, her mind churning. She couldn't stop thinking about the note in Chloe's pocket.

"I think we're done here," Monty said, holding her eyes. "You spoke to one of her friends, didn't you? We need to speak to the others."

"And search their rooms as well," Nikki said, a grim tone in her voice. "Let's hope we don't find anything similar in their rooms."

"Do you want to start that now?" Monty asked.

"No time like the present. If you could please get the team together, I'd like to meet them downstairs."

"Aye, aye, captain." Monty gave a mock salute, and made for the door. "I'll also speak to Mr Flint downstairs. I think he's got in touch with Chloe's other friends."

"You do that." Nikki smiled. After Monty left, she looked around the room, her thoughts running loops. What was Chloe up to? Was she really dealing in drugs? Or had someone planted them here? Could it be her boyfriend, Mark, stashing them here?

She pulled out her phone and called Nish.

"Yes, guv," Nish answered.

"Can you ask the researchers at the nick to look at Chloe's social media and feed back to us? I want to get an idea about her lifestyle."

"No problem, guv."

ELEVEN

Nikki went down the staircase, and as she walked down the ground floor hallway, she looked out through the elaborate arches that flanked the view to the garden. New College had some avant garde works of modern art, and Nikki watched them absentmindedly as she strode across the hallway and out into the quad. The students were out and about, and she got curious glances from them.

Monty was chatting with Nish outside the forensic tent. Nikki cast a glance towards the tent, but didn't go inside.

"Has Dr Raman gone?"

"Yes, and the victim's at the morgue," Nish said. "The Piersons are en route to the morgue to identify the body. Dr Raman said the postmortem report should be ready tomorrow afternoon."

"Okay. Did you check with the researchers about Chloe's social media?"

"Yes, they've forwarded the links to Kristy." Nish turned around, looking for her, and then pointed towards the porters' lodge. Kristy was walking up to them.

"Have you heard?" Nish asked Kristy, who looked mystified.

Monty said, "I've told Nish about the cocaine in Chloe's room." He updated Kristy as well, whose jaw dropped.

"That's more than she needed for a night out."

"You need about that much when you're out, eh?" Nish said teasingly.

"Shut it," Kristy said. She pulled out her phone as she got closer to them. "Lisa sent me these." Lisa was one of the researchers. "Looks like Chloe was quite the party animal," she said. They stood around Kristy as she flicked through the images on Chloe's social media.

They showed Chloe with a group of other young people inside a bar, drinking, and walking down the street.

"That's the High Street, near the Covered Market," Nish said. Nikki and the others agreed.

More photos showed Kristy hugging an Afro Caribbean man, and a kissing selfie with him. The tagged name on the photo was Mark Ofori.

"Now we have a visual of Mark," Nikki said. "That's good."

Nikki noted Chloe wasn't into expensive clothes, or glam makeup, she had more of a hippie chic vibe. Kristy stopped scrolling at a photo of Chloe with Jemima, Mark, and a couple of other women outside a building with a big, blue neon sign that said *Cargo*.

Nish said, "I've heard of this place. It's a big club near the train station. Popular with students and townies." He asked Kristy to check the date of the photo. It was two weeks ago, on a Thursday.

"That would be the student night, so they'd get cheap drinks and entry."

"Make some calls to see if you can speak to the owners, and check CCTV on the nights Chloe was there."

"Will do." Nish glanced at Nikki. "Shall we take swabs

from everyone, guv? The porters, groundsman, and the victim's friends?"

"Absolutely," Nikki said approvingly. "And don't forget Mr Flint, and Chloe's college tutor. You might not be able to swab them all today, but try your best. And get their phone numbers as well. Ask the uniforms to help you."

She continued, "Make sure we have the CCTV footage from the porters' lodge, and from all the street entrances."

Monty said, "One of the uniforms can take Chloe's laptop to the cyber crimes lab. And the other stuff we found in her room."

Nikki turned to Monty. "Good. Now then, let's get to those interviews before we lose the day."

Monty called Mr Flint and he informed her that Sally Usborne and Fiona Bartlett were in Sally's room and gave the room number.

Nikki and Monty walked in silence, heading for the quad.

"Jemima wasn't much help," Monty said. "She's too scared or too torn up to think straight."

"Yeah," Nikki replied, her voice flat. "But Sally and Fiona should be able to give us more. They were also close to Chloe..."

"You think they'll talk?"

Nikki sighed. "I don't know. But we need to push them."

They reached the residential hall where Sally Usborne lived, in the same building where Chloe and Jemima had their rooms. They climbed up to the third floor and Monty knocked firmly on the door of room 304. After a few moments, the door opened a fraction, then wider.

A woman stood in the doorway, her blonde hair messy, her eyes red from crying. She looked fragile. Behind her, a young brunette sat on the bed, her arms crossed tightly over her knees. She too looked bedraggled, hair in clumps, eyes blank and unfocused.

"Are you the detectives?" the blonde woman asked.

"Yes." Nikki showed her warrant card. "What's your name?"

"Sally Usborne." Sally pointed to the brunette on the bed. "That's Fiona."

Fiona glanced at Nikki once, then looked away swiftly.

"Thanks for seeing us," Nikki said, stepping into the room. She glanced around briefly. The room was neat, almost sterile, as though Sally had been trying to keep everything in its place while her world fell apart.

Monty stayed near the door, his eyes fixed on Fiona, who hadn't moved. Nikki took a seat on the only chair in the room, facing the two girls. There was no point in small talk; they needed to get to the heart of this.

"Sally, Fiona, we need to talk about Chloe," Nikki began, her tone firm but not unkind. "I know this is hard, but we need to know what happened last night. We need to know about her life, her relationships. Anything that could help us understand what led to her falling."

Sally looked down at her hands, twisting them in her lap. Fiona's gaze remained steady, unreadable.

"We already told you," Sally said quietly. "We saw her around six p.m. She seemed... fine. She didn't say much, just that she might go out."

"Go out where?" Monty asked. He had shut the door, and his tall frame was leaning against it, head resting above the door frame.

Sally shook her head. "She didn't say. Chloe didn't always tell us where she was going. She was... private about some things."

"Like what?" Nikki leaned forward, watching Sally closely. "What was she private about?"

The hesitation was brief but telling. Sally glanced at Fiona, who remained silent, then back at Nikki. "She just didn't talk about certain things. Like who she was seeing. What she was doing outside of college. We didn't ask too many questions."

Nikki's eyes narrowed. This wasn't unusual for university students, but the vagueness was setting off alarms. "Was Chloe involved in anything dangerous? Drugs, maybe?"

Both girls stiffened at the question. Fiona shifted uncomfortably, her eyes darting to Sally before quickly looking away.

"I don't know what you're talking about," Sally said, her voice too quick, too defensive. "Chloe wasn't like that."

"Are you sure?" Monty's voice was low, calm, but the edge of suspicion was clear. He glanced at Nikki, and she inclined her head a fraction. It was time to be open with the girls.

Monty continued. "Because we have reason to believe otherwise. We know Chloe was involved with drugs."

Sally's face went pale, her eyes wide with shock. Fiona, for the first time, looked genuinely rattled. She stared at Nikki, her mouth slightly open as if she were about to speak but didn't know what to say.

"You knew, didn't you?" Nikki pressed, her gaze never leaving their faces. "You knew Chloe was into drugs."

Sally's lower lip quivered, and tears welled up in her eyes. She looked like she was about to break, but Fiona was the one who spoke first.

"We didn't know," Fiona said, her voice sharp, defensive. "We... we had our suspicions. But Chloe never told us anything. She kept it secret from us."

"But you knew something," Monty said. "You were close to her. You must've talked about it."

Sally sniffed, wiping at her eyes with the back of her hand. "She never told us what she was doing, in that way," she whispered.

Nikki watched Sally carefully. The guilt was written all over her face, but there was still more. She could feel it. "What about Mark Ofori?" Nikki asked, shifting gears. "You said Chloe was seeing someone. Was it Mark?"

Both girls froze. Sally's eyes widened again, and Fiona's face hardened.

"Yes, she was," Fiona said, her tone flat. Her hard eyes glittered as she looked back at Nikki. "Not a crime, is it?"

Nikki wondered why Fiona had her back up. The girl was angry about something, and she wanted to know why. She also didn't like the way the girls seemed to be on edge when Mark's name was mentioned.

"I didn't say that," Nikki said. "We just want to know more about Mark."

Fiona's jaw clenched, but Sally spoke up, her voice shaky. "She never introduced us to him. We only knew about him from what she told us. She said she was in love. That they were going out, but it was... new."

Nikki exchanged a glance with Monty.

"Did Chloe go out with Mark last night?" Nikki asked, her tone gentle but probing. "Is that where she went after dinner?"

Sally's shoulders sagged, and fresh tears spilled down her cheeks. Fiona looked away, her face tight with emotion.

"I don't know," Sally said, her voice barely above a whisper. "She didn't say. But it wouldn't surprise me if she did."

Nikki's mind raced. Chloe was leading a double life – one as a university student, the other in the murky world of drugs and clubbing. And now this Mark Ofori was in the middle of it all. They needed to find him, and fast.

"What kind of person is Mark?" Monty asked. "Was he involved with drugs, too?"

Fiona shook her head quickly. "We don't know," she said, her voice strained. "Chloe never talked about him like that. She just said he liked to go clubbing, that he was... fun. But we don't know anything else. She didn't share those parts of her life with us."

"But you knew," Nikki said, her eyes locking onto Fiona's. "You knew Chloe was in deep with something dangerous. You just didn't want to admit it."

Fiona's eyes flickered with something – guilt, fear, anger, Nikki couldn't tell which. But before she could push further, Sally broke down completely.

"We didn't know what to do!" Sally sobbed, her hands covering her face. "We knew something was wrong, but Chloe... she was always so strong. She acted like she had everything under control, like she didn't need our help."

Fiona put a hand on Sally's back, rubbing it gently. "We tried to talk to her," she said quietly. "We told her to be careful. But Chloe was stubborn. She didn't listen."

"Look," Nikki said, softening her tone. "We need to find out what happened to Chloe. And we can't do that if you're holding back. If you know anything else – anything at all – you need to tell us."

Sally sniffed again, wiping her eyes. "We've told you everything we know," she said, her voice small.

"Are you sure?" Monty pressed, his gaze shifting from Sally to Fiona.

Fiona looked away, her jaw clenched tight. But Sally's tears had stopped, and she stared up at Monty with wide, frightened eyes. Nikki could see the cracks forming.

"Please," Nikki said softly. "Help us. Help Chloe."

The silence stretched on, heavy and suffocating. Then, finally, Sally nodded.

"There's... something else," she whispered.

Fiona stiffened beside her, but Sally ignored her, her eyes fixed on Nikki's. "Chloe said Mark was into some things. He liked partying, clubbing. And we think maybe... maybe that's how she got involved with the drugs. We never saw anything, but we heard her talk about it. About him. He was into that lifestyle. And Chloe... she followed him."

Fiona gave Sally a withering look. She cut her eyes at Nikki. "Chloe didn't just follow him. She was into the party lifestyle already. She was one of the founding members of TITS."

"So you think Chloe was getting deeper into that lifestyle? Was she doing anything dangerous?" Nikki prompted. But both girls were quiet now. Sally shrugged, and Fiona ignored them.

Nikki's mind raced. Chloe had been pulled into something dangerous, something she couldn't control. And now she was dead.

"What else do you know about Mark?"

Nikki was interested in Fiona's reactions and rested her eyes on her. Fiona stared at her for a few seconds, then looked away.

"If you know anything else, now is the time to tell us."

Sally spoke in a small voice. "He's a law student at Balliol."

"Yes, we know. And he lives in Summertown. Is that correct?"

Both girls nodded, but didn't say anything more. Fiona still remained aloof and defensive. Nikki got the impression they didn't want to talk about Mark. And it was Fiona who was holding back, and perhaps forcing Sally to do the same.

"Thank you for your time," Nikki said, her voice steady. "We'll be in touch if we need anything else."

Monty said, "Please don't leave Oxford. We might want to speak to you again. If you remember anything else, please give us a call."

The girls nodded, their faces pale, their eyes hollow. Nikki gave Fiona one last look, then got up. Sally shut the door behind them. They walked away, but then Nikki doubled back, and tiptoed to the room. She put her ear to the door. She could hear urgent whispers inside. The voices got louder, and then she heard Fiona.

"How could you tell them that? How?" Fiona shouted. Sally was crying again.

"I'm sorry," Sally whimpered. "But they need to know."

"About Mark? Why? He's not responsible for what happened to Chloe, is he?"

"You don't know that!" Sally shouted back, then sobbed.

"Keep your voice down," Fiona said.

Then it was quiet, but Nikki heard them whispering. She listened, but couldn't make out the words. Then the girls were silent.

Nikki tiptoed back to the end of the corridor, where Monty was waiting. They went into the stairs landing, and descended the ancient stone staircase slowly.

"What did you hear?" Monty asked in a low voice.

"Fiona's holding back about Mark. Sally wanted to tell us more, I think. We need to speak to Mark ASAP."

"Why should Fiona care about Mark?" Monty asked, and they exchanged a look.

"She might have the hots for him," Nikki mused, deep in thought. "There could be a love triangle here. Fiona might be protecting Mark."

As they walked out towards the exit and the porters' lodge, Nikki's phone pinged. It was Patmore, and she answered.

"I got your message about the note in the victim's pocket. Is this true?"

Nikki had a sense of foreboding, and her heart beat faster. "Yes, sir, it is."

"Come to my office, now. We need to sort this out. Where is the note?"

Monty said, "In my pocket, in an evidence bag, sir."

"Good. I want to see it."

TWELVE

"What the hell is this about?"

Nikki had been summoned back to the station by her superior, Detective Superintendent Dean Patmore, who was now jabbing at the note inside the plastic specimen bag on his desk. "Could it be a prank?"

The air in the room was stuffy, thanks to Patmore's twenty-a-day smoking habit. The odour of nicotine and tar seemed to coat the furniture and carpets.

Nikki knew he didn't believe it could be a prank. Someone had to know she would be involved in the case – or at least that she worked for Thames Valley Police.

"It would have to be a prankster from inside the force, then... and I don't think that's possible," Nikki said. "Monty suggested an OCN link? I helped take down an Albanian gang in London. They were heavily into cocaine importing, amongst other substances. Given what we found in the victim's room, it makes sense. But personally, I don't see it."

"What did you find in the victim's room?"

"A stash of cocaine and ecstasy pills. Enough to be a supplier. It wasn't just for her personal use."

"OCNs have county lines. A gang in London wouldn't be distributing in this region. They'd be trampling on another OCN's turf."

"That's what I thought as well, sir. I think we can rule out the OCN angle."

Patmore reached for his packet of cigarettes, then cursed softly and sat back. With nicotine-stained fingers, he rubbed his clean-shaven jaw.

"The uniforms were first on the scene, right? And a PCSO too?"

"Yes, we've spoken to them already. They didn't see anyone leaving a note."

"Someone put that note in her pocket. Or gave it to her..." Monty glanced at Patmore, then at Nikki. "But DI Gill doesn't know the woman, or any of her friends."

Nikki shook her head. "I've racked my brains, but no, I don't."

Patmore coughed. "Well, get cracking. But I don't like it. Has anyone else apart from you two seen this note? We don't want the media getting involved."

Nikki sighed in relief. "No, sir, the uniforms didn't get close enough to see the note. I believe we were the first to spot it."

"Good. Keep it between you two for now."

"I need to tell my team, sir. Just the two DCs. They won't tell anyone – I trust them."

"Okay." Patmore coughed, hacking up phlegm. Nikki was disgusted and looked away. That was one aspect of a smoker's life she could never get used to. Patmore spat into a tissue and tossed it into the bin. He drawled in his low, gravelly voice.

"The press will be on this like flies on shite. We need some answers, and quick. Send me a report by tonight."

. . .

Back in the office, Nikki opened up her laptop and checked her emails. Nikki ran a search on the police database for Chloe, her parents, and her friends. Nothing. It seemed that no one Nikki had met today had a criminal record – nor had any Penalty Charge Notices filed against them.

The door opened, and the two detective constables walked in. Kristy held the door open for Nish, who was carrying a tray with cups of coffee and biscuits.

"We've come bearing gifts," Kristy said.

"Well done." Nikki smiled, accepting her skinny latte with a murmur of thanks.

Kristy and Nish sat down at their desks. "We got Mark Ofori's address from Mr Flint, who called Balliol College Student Affairs. On the way back, we decided to stop by Mark's house in Summertown," Nish said. "He wasn't in, but one of his housemates said they'd let him know. Mark's not answering his phone."

"That's strange," Nikki said. "How many times have you tried his phone?"

"More than five times. I sent a text as well. He hasn't replied yet. I didn't tell him what's happened to Chloe, just asked him to get in touch. Nothing so far," Nish shrugged.

"And his housemate seemed a bit shifty," Kristy added. "He looked like he'd just got out of bed, and it's almost midday. His name's Chris Matthews, but he's not a student. He works in advertising, apparently." Kristy frowned at Nikki. "Are there advertising firms in Oxford?"

"Did you ask him where he worked?" Nikki asked.

"Yes. He gave me the name of some agency. I need to check it out. Anyway, Chris said he'd seen Chloe with Mark a couple of times and vaguely remembered her. He didn't know her well, and we didn't tell him much."

"And we don't know when Mark's getting back?"

Both Kristy and Nish shook their heads.

"Have you asked Traffic to check when his phone was last used? We might have to triangulate his signal."

"I can do that now," Kristy said, reaching for her phone. There was a knock on the door, and Monty entered, ducking slightly so he didn't hit his head.

"Started without me?" Monty said.

"Got a cappuccino for you, guv," Nish said, indicating the tray. Monty thanked him and picked up a chocolate bourbon biscuit, which he dunked in the coffee. He sat down in the chair opposite Nikki's desk.

"Anything new?" he asked, glancing at Nish and Kristy.

"We didn't find Mark Ofori," Nish said, "but we're triangulating the last signal from his phone now."

"He's just a student, for crying out loud," Monty said. "We shouldn't have to track him. But it is worrying," he conceded, locking eyes with Nikki. "Especially if he had anything to do with that stash in Chloe's room."

"My sentiments exactly," Nikki said, taking a long sip of her coffee.

Monty tapped the tabletop with a long finger. "Fiona Bartlett was acting strangely, don't you think? She looked well pissed off."

"And on edge," Nikki said. "I'm not sure what's bothering her. None of the girls have a police record, but we need to investigate Fiona carefully. She lives in Cowley, doesn't she?"

"Yes," Monty replied. He pulled out a small black leather notebook from the inside pocket of his jacket. "I've got her address here. And her phone number. Shall we arrange a meeting or drop in unannounced?"

"Just call her." Nikki sighed. "Let's not waste time chasing. If she starts avoiding us, then we bring her in."

"Right," Nikki said, standing up and going to the whiteboard. She pulled out a black marker. "Let's make a timeline," she said.

"Chloe was last seen yesterday evening, around six p.m. She went to her room when she and Jemima got back from their tutorial. We don't know what Chloe had been doing earlier that day – probably the usual student activities, either in the library or at the gym. She then went out after dinner, and we don't know where or with whom. Sally and Fiona think it might have been with Mark, but we're not sure."

Kristy said, "Traffic are already scanning CCTV with facial recognition software. Hopefully, they'll get a hit somewhere in town. There are cameras everywhere."

"If she was in town," Nikki reminded her. "We don't know that yet. Have Traffic looked at CCTV outside New College?"

"They're going through it as we speak."

"That might give us an indication of which direction she was headed. But in any case, Chloe wasn't seen for the rest of the evening. The porters' lodge said she came back late, but we don't know the exact time. She had to get back inside the college to go up onto the ramparts. Was she alone?"

Monty added, "And what were the sounds the porter, Chris Dooley, heard inside the grounds?"

"Some students came back late from a nightclub and had a smoking session on the college grounds?" Nish suggested.

"That's more than likely. In which case, the girls we interviewed should have known something. But they denied it, so I wonder if they're hiding something," Nikki said.

Monty interjected, "I think so too. Fiona looked angry with Sally, didn't she? And when you went back and listened through the door, Fiona shouted at her."

"Her exact words were, 'How could you tell them that?' As if Sally had betrayed them."

Nikki wrote on the whiteboard again. "The time of death was around two a.m. Chloe falls to her death from the rampart wall. She has no other trauma, apart from the impact when her head hit the ground, and she dies. That's all we know so far."

She scanned her team members. Monty said, "It's too early to have suspects, but we obviously have her friends – and Mark, in particular. But what bothers me the most is the stash of street drugs in her room. That cocaine was pure. Uncut. Street dealers would kill to get hold of it. They usually cut it with sodium bicarb, talcum powder, anything to stretch it out. That block is worth more than a hundred grand if you ask me."

"Which OCNs are active in the narcotics market here?" Nikki asked.

"When I was at North Kidlington HQ," Monty said, "the Botley Road Boys were active. I heard last week one of their senior members was caught in Cowley after a year-long surveillance operation."

"I wouldn't be surprised if the stash we found in Chloe's room came from them."

"Let's track them down," Nikki said. "If Chloe had links to the Botley Road Boys, I want to know."

THIRTEEN

Eighteen years ago

Constance could hear the voices again. They spoke in whispers, but she could hear them. She had told Jeffrey, and his suggestion was to take her to the doctors. He didn't understand. These people were real, and they were making her life a misery.

Constance, or Connie, as she was known, heard her toddler make a sound as she slept. Little Chloe was fast asleep, her tiny, chubby fists tucked under her chin. Jeff was out with his mates in the pub. Yes, that's how much he cared about her. Or was she being too harsh?

Yes, you are, the woman's shrill voice said. *You mess everything up. Look what happened with your last boyfriend.*

Her friend, another female voice, but with a Scottish accent, replied. *Don't even bother with her anymore. Have you seen her hair? She looks like a bloody badger. Maybe she can't go to the shops to buy some dye.*

Connie heard them through the walls. They were next door, and she didn't have the guts to face them. Sometimes, she heard them on TV. She'd be sitting there, and the women on TV became these two. They criticised her constantly.

Connie picked up the phone and called the man. He was the only one who could help her at times like these. She couldn't hide the panic in her voice.

"Hi. Yes, it's me. I'm not... I can hear the voices again. They keep coming back. I don't know what to do."

His voice was calm and authoritative. "Did you take the medicine?"

Connie trembled. "I did. But this time, it made the voices worse."

"Hmm. You might have to take it like the last time." He had injected the medication, as he called it, into her elbow vein. Minutes later, Connie had felt a delicious calm descend on her. She felt like she was floating on a cloud, without a care in the world. The voices had gone, and her anxiety was long forgotten. She could just close her eyes and feel peace. He had taken her clothes off, and they had been intimate then, although she didn't really feel like it. She felt guilty as she thought she was cheating on Jeffrey. But she didn't have the strength to stop him. She was past caring.

Since then, he had had this strange hold on her. He had given her the medicine as a little ball that she could ingest. It tasted bitter. It didn't work as well as the injection had.

"Come to my place. I can give you the injection."

Connie heard the front door open downstairs. Jeffrey was back from the pub. "I can't now," she said in a hurried whisper. "My husband's back. Maybe tomorrow."

"Wait till he's asleep. Then come out. I'll be waiting at the end of the road at one a.m."

Connie hung up without replying. She listened as Jeffrey pottered around downstairs, then came up. He went into his room, the main bedroom. Then she heard his steps outside her door. She wanted to sleep here with Chloe. The toddler's sounds were comforting. When she listened to Chloe breathe, she felt quieter in her mind. She didn't feel the same when she was next to Jeffrey.

"Connie," Jeffrey whispered softly. "Are you awake?"

Connie watched the closed door, and the light spilling out from the corners. It looked weird, like the palms of a dark hand surrounded by shafts of yellow light. She'd locked it, and Jeffrey couldn't open it. The door handle went down as Jeffrey tried to open the door. Connie's heart beat faster.

"Connie," Jeffrey whispered once again. Then he appeared to realise she was asleep. He walked away. The landing light went off. Connie stared at the closed door, heart beating in her mouth, the loud thumps like explosions in her head. Chloe stirred in her sleep, and her sounds were a welcome distraction. Chloe was waving her hands in the air, but her eyes were still closed.

Connie turned her phone light on but directed it to the floor so it wouldn't fall on Chloe's eyes. She patted Chloe gently and cooed at her, and the little one rubbed her eyes, and turned over to sleep on her chest. She liked doing that, and Connie let her. She had read somewhere that cot deaths happened when babies slept on their backs. She had fixated on it and had visited the doctor almost daily till Jeffrey had to get involved. Connie's never-ending anxiety made her do these things.

Chloe fell back asleep again. Connie turned the light off and sat down on the bed next to the cot. One of the voices chirped up again.

She's such a horrible mother. Never breastfed her child. That's why the baby doesn't sleep well at night.

Connie clasped her hands over her ears. She went closer to Chloe's cot, so she could hear her breathing. Normally, that helped. She had a little respite, then the other, Scottish voice whispered:

That's why she'll never know any peace.

Connie grit her teeth, and slammed her fist against her thigh. Then a teardrop of grief and frustration trickled out of her eye and coursed down her cheek. She looked at her phone. He had sent her a message.

> I'll be waiting. One a.m. Usual place.

Her fingers hovered over the phone, then she made up her mind. His medicine was the only thing that made her forget about the world.

> If I can make it, I'll see you there. Wait for me. If I can't, I'll let you know.

Connie had met the man at the pub, when she was having a drink with her friend Clarissa. He had approached their table, and Clarissa had known him. She said they'd had a relationship a while ago, and then broke up. The man had caught Connie's attention immediately. She met him again, outside a café. This time, they talked, and then they met again.

Connie felt guilty for meeting a man and not telling Jeffrey. But the man understood her problems. He had been through similar troubles. He told her about them like only a fellow sufferer could. She couldn't talk to Jeffrey like this. He was always an outsider.

But her new man... he belonged in that dark, monstrous world. He knew what hearing voices was like. And he had the medicine to stop it from happening.

Connie waited for a while. She couldn't sleep. The doctors gave her tablets that made her drowsy at night. But even when she took them, she was groggy in the daytime. Now, she would sleep in the day when Chloe had her nap. But the mornings were hellish – she had to drag herself through a thornbush in order to survive. Chloe went to nursery, and Connie came home and slumped into bed.

Connie opened the door softly and tiptoed out. She knew where the loose floorboards were. She put an ear on the bedroom door and heard Jeffrey snoring. She stole downstairs and put her jacket on. It was freezing outside. She locked the door with barely any sound and hurried to the end of the road. The cars had a sheen of white frost on them; the air made cloudy question marks in front of her face. She saw his car. He kept the engine and lights off. She slipped into the front seat.

"I don't have long. Chloe's sleeping."

"Good to see you," he muttered. His face remained in the darkness, and she could only see his outline. His thin cheeks were like granite. He reached out a hand and brushed his fingers down her face. Connie shivered.

He started the car, and they drove to the park a few blocks away. There was an area of the car park where trees branches leaned over the cars. He parked there. Without a word, they went to the back seat. He had the tourniquet and prepared syringe in his pocket. She held the phone light as he worked. The tourniquet went around her elbow, and she clenched and unclenched her fist several time. The blue vein in her elbow stood up, proud.

"Relax. Don't look. Sharp sting, now, okay?"

She nodded, and leaned back on the seat. She jolted as the needle pricked her skin. The sudden, sharp pain was lost in the rush of the warm liquid mingling into her bloodstream. She felt her heart rate kick up, and then the booming feeling as the drug coursed through her body. She breathed faster, her eyes popping open. Then the rush subsided, and slowly, the glorious peace smothered her eyelids, covering her like a cocoon. The voices faded, then disappeared completely.

She felt his lips on hers, and his hands moving under her dress, cupping her breasts.

"I need to go back home," she mumbled.

"Soon, my love," he whispered. "Soon."

FOURTEEN

Nikki and Monty were finishing up a late lunch in the canteen when Nish came in. They were seated at the back, but Monty saw Nish at the doorway, looking around, and waved him over. Nish approached, an excited look on his face.

"We've got the CCTV from New College. Do you want to have a look?"

Nikki took a quick gulp of water. "What about CCTV around the High Street?"

"Yep, we've got that too. Kristy is already going through it. Shall I see you back at the office?"

"Yes, see you there."

Nikki's phone beeped, and it was her sixteen-year-old daughter, Rita. She was checking how Nikki was and if she could still come to Oxford the next weekend. Rita lived in London with her dad and visited Nikki every other weekend. She also stayed with Nikki for half of the school holidays and half-terms, a time Nikki treasured.

It wasn't ideal – Nikki missed her like mad. But Rita was sixteen now, and her life and school were in south-west London. Nikki couldn't get a job around there, and she needed a break from London's gritty streets. She consoled herself with the fact that Rita was happy, and they still had regular contact.

Yes, of course, Nikki texted back. *All okay with you?*

Rita replied with a combination of thumbs-up and heart-shaped emojis. Nikki smiled at the screen, then put the phone back in her coat.

"I heard back from my colleague at North Kidlington HQ," Monty said. "The Botley Road Boys aren't just active, they've spread all around Oxford and even into the Cotswolds. He said the stash of drugs we found is more than likely linked to the gang. Not good news."

"No, not good at all," Nikki breathed. "Come on, let's go check the CCTV."

They went back to the office, and Kristy was ready with a laptop. She showed them the grainy black-and-white footage from outside the New College gates. The porters' lodge was visible, and every now and then students came and went. It was time stamped 18.30. Kristy stopped the tape when they saw a young woman step out. She was about five feet six inches, with brown hair, and wore a pink cardigan with a light dark-blue jacket, blue jeans and white trainers.

The clothing matched the description of Chloe Pierson, and her face was recognisable. She nodded at Kristy, and the detective constable played the tape again. They watched as Chloe walked down the road and took a right turn.

Kristy changed screens and brought up CCTV from a different set of cameras. These were operated by the Oxford City Council. Nikki knew the team had done very well to get the footage so quickly. The screen now showed four boxes, each displaying a different angle of the High Street. Chloe had been identified with a red circle. They watched as she walked down a side street and into Holywell Street, the main road behind New College.

Chloe walked further, approaching Magdalene College and

the bridge over the River Cherwell. The bridge was a busy road, with cars and pedestrians on the pavement. Just before the bridge, a side access sloped down to a few lovely pubs by the riverfront. Rowing and punting were common on the Cherwell. Chloe took that road and disappeared again.

Half an hour later, she reappeared. This time she was with a man.

"That looks like Mark Ofori," Nikki said, pointing at the screen. Kristy froze the image and zoomed in on the man's face. She used image recognition software to copy his face and then pasted it into the database. Within seconds, they had a match from a driving licence and a newspaper article. There was no doubt – it was Mark Ofori.

"Show me the newspaper article," Nikki said. She squinted at the screen, wondering why she hadn't seen this before.

The headline read:

Turnham High School Student Expelled for Alleged Drug Dealing.

There was a close-up photo of Mark's face, taken from his passport. Nikki scanned the first few sentences. There was no mention of police involvement or an arrest, which tallied with what she had discovered earlier. Mark didn't have a police record. But it was interesting, she thought, that despite his chequered academic history, he was still allowed into Oxford.

Monty said, "Turnham High School is a prestigious, fee-paying school in Cheltenham. If he went there, he's either very clever or has rich parents."

Nikki shook her head. "He doesn't have a father, and his mother is a healthcare assistant at the local hospital. They live in Slough. I don't think he comes from a rich family."

"Must be brains, then," Kristy said. "Otherwise, he wouldn't be in Oxford."

"After getting expelled from Turnham College?" Nikki raised her eyebrows. "He must be a genius."

Nikki made a note to herself to dig deeper into Mark.

Kristy played the footage again. They watched as Mark and Chloe crossed the bridge quickly and walked into the busy streets of Cowley. Here, the cameras lost them.

"What happened?" Nikki asked.

"CCTV dark spots," Kristy replied. "We don't see Chloe again until her return to the college."

She switched screens and showed footage from the New College cameras. At 00:30, Chloe came back alone. Her gait was different this time, Nikki noticed. She skipped along, then stumbled and fell. She stood up and did a twirl.

"Had a few drinks, clearly," Kristy muttered.

They watched as Chloe went inside the college gates and disappeared from view again. Kristy was about to close the screen, but Nikki stopped her.

"I want to see who comes in afterwards."

Kristy fast-forwarded the footage, and just ten minutes later, a group of students arrived, clearly drunk and in good spirits. They went in through the gates as well.

"Is this the group that made the sounds the porters heard later on?" Nikki asked. "Identify them and speak to them. They might know what happened to Chloe or have seen her that night."

"Got it, guv," Kristy said.

Nish nudged her elbow. "Show the earlier footage of Chloe out and about in town. Traffic got hold of Chloe's movements going back two weeks."

Kristy nodded and pulled up the files on her laptop. The screen was divided into four boxes again, but with different dates and times. Each showed a different part of Oxford town, and a place also outside. Nikki squinted at the lower left box.

"Where is that? The street's quieter. Not Kidlington, is it?"

"Nope, that's Iffley. She took the bus there, and she's just getting off it now." Kristy played the coloured image and they watched as Chloe stepped out of the bus station and walked down the road. A river became visible on the right. Nikki recognised Iffley Lock, a landmark from the seventeenth century. Iffley was a quiet village in southern Oxford.

Chloe crossed the road and went down the towpath of the river. Kristy fast-forwarded, and a different film played, showing Chloe walking down the High Street. A market was in progress, and they watched as she stepped inside a stall. The stall's awning prevented any further views. Chloe came out and walked around the stalls, then disappeared from view.

"Apart from the High Street," Nish said, "there isn't much CCTV coverage around Iffley. Chloe must've walked around."

"And the market changes location, by the way," Kristy added. "It's held on the church grounds, sometimes. Any CCTV there?"

"Nope," Nish said. "I checked with Traffic. In Iffley the CCTV is mainly on the High Street, and around the Lock."

"But residents will have their own security cameras," Monty commented.

They all knew how useful personal cameras could be catching a burglar, or someone who ran down the street. Even dashcam footage from cars could be critical in solving a case.

"When was this?"

"This was twenty eighth of May, guv. At 15.45 hours."

"So she left Mark in Cowley, and went to Iffley on her own," Nikki mused thoughtfully.

"Go further back. See if you can find how often she went to Iffley. College students don't often go there, correct?" She looked at the others.

Monty regarded her with hooded eyes. "Why don't you tell us?" he suggested. "Since you're such an expert on Oxford."

She narrowed her eyes at him. He was getting back to her about her previous remarks of growing up in Oxford.

"I think," Nikki said with emphasis, "that students like spending time around the bars of Oxford and Cowley. Maybe Jericho as well. When did you attend Oxford University?"

"Oh, I'd say working for the Thames Valley Police for twelve years kind of helps knowing about what sort of crimes students get up to, you know?" Monty winked at Nikki. "Yes, you're right. Iffley's a sleepy old village, and not many students go there. Though it's not that far from Cowley." He turned to the constables. "Was Chloe on her own when she went to Iffley?"

"Yes." Kristy had picked up another file, arranged by date. She played the footage. It was from the twenty-ninth of May. It showed Chloe going into Iffley High Street again, where the market was in progress.

"She goes into that same stall. What for?"

Kristy shrugged, and fast-forwarded the tape. It followed Chloe, but she vanished from view when she went down a side street.

"Find out how often she went to Iffley, and who set up that stall," Nikki instructed. "That won't be easy, but there must be a market organisation, like a farmer's committee."

Nish said, "She must've gone there for a reason. Not just to shop in the market stalls. There are plenty of markets all around Oxford. The Covered Market is permanent, and right next to all the colleges."

"I'll check," Kristy said.

"Detective Inspector." The cheerful voice of their head of scene of crime, Hetty Burford, piped up from behind them.

"Cometh the hour, cometh the lady," Nicki replied warmly.

Hetty's eyes were theatrical as she cooed at them, "Wait till you see what I've got in my box of goodies." She tapped the slim plastic folder in her hand and pulled out pieces of A4 paper, placing them in front of them.

"As you can see, I've been working extra hard. I deserve some cookies." Hetty winked at Nikki. She made no secret of her fondness for the sugary stuff. "These are preliminary reports," Hetty said, growing serious. The others picked up copies from the table.

"As you can see," Hetty said, "there's no fingerprint match on IDENT1. Chloe didn't have any PCNs or a police record. She didn't have any other names. Born and raised in the UK."

Nish nodded. "Yes, that's right."

"On her fingers, there's some DNA from another person. No matches on the criminal database. There's nothing under her nails. Dr Raman also mentioned that she didn't struggle or fight with anyone. That's when we tend to get skin cells under the nails. Do we have DNA samples from her friends and boyfriend?"

"Boyfriend is missing," Nikki said. She looked at the constables, and Kristy answered.

"We've taken DNA swabs from everyone at the college who knew her. I've sent them to you."

"Right, so no matches there. The DNA on Chloe's hands must belong to someone else. Her partner, maybe."

Hetty continued, "There's chocolate on her fingertips. She'd been eating recently. She also had chocolate wrappers in her coat pocket. Nothing surprising there, but I've sent them for further analysis and toxicology, via Dr Raman. She will alert us when the results, if any, are back.

"Faint traces of nicotine on the fingers as well. Chloe liked occasional cigarettes. Cocaine from her nose swabs, and on the fingertips as well. She had dabbled recently, in the last two to three days."

"Not surprising," Monty said. "We found a big stash in her room."

"And that's getting looked at now. There's a logo on the packet, and we're looking for a match.

"Her hair follicles also show various chemicals. As you know, hairs are routinely used these days for drug tests. I got cocaine obviously, and some MDMA. They stay in the system for a good few days. She might not have taken any recently. I found some other chemicals as well. Again, these have been sent for toxicology."

"We can't wait four days for tox to come back..." Nikki said. "I'll speak to Dr Raman to expedite them. We need an answer tomorrow."

Hetty nodded. "At the crime scene, apart from Chloe's blood and DNA, we found nothing else. Boot prints of the porters, policemen, but not near the body. And before you ask, none of the boot prints have shown a match on the database."

"Good. You deserved more than a cookie. How about a doughnut?"

"Now you're talking. When is the postmortem due?"

"Sheila should have it done tomorrow. Hopefully, we can get the tox back then as well, with some pressure. And let's do some more digging into Mark Ofori. Something doesn't feel right about him."

FIFTEEN

Eight weeks ago

Chloe Pierson put her hand on the attic ladder and stepped on the first rung. The black square of the attic opening loomed over her head. It had been years since she'd been up there. Today, she wanted to show Mark, her boyfriend, some old photos of when she was a child.

"Be careful," Mark said behind her. "Do you want me to go first?"

"I've done this before," Chloe said. Then she thought of the spiders. She hated spiders but didn't like killing them. And all their webs would get caught in her hair. Maybe she should let Mark go ahead. But then she steeled herself.

"I'll be fine," she said, more to herself than to Mark. She went up and found the light switch next to the hatch door. She squinted up at the cone of yellow light that appeared over her head. The attic was dusty, and she flinched as she waved away the cobwebs. The rafters were dark outlines behind the light. She looked at the dark shadows in the corners – boxes and suitcases left and forgotten. For some reason, they looked foreboding. Chloe shook her head, trying to dispel the sudden gloom that come over her, brushing it off like the old cobwebs. She wanted to show Mark photos of Connie, her mother, and herself. Them together – which she had only known in photos, never in real life. That odd feeling of missing something she'd never had swept through her again. She stepped carefully over the pile of rolled-up carpets and boxes on the floor.

Mark followed behind her and helped move a couple of suitcases. Chloe crouched down and flipped open a large plastic box. Inside lay her mother's clothes and jewellery that Chloe had last looked at when she was a teenager. With her father, she had gone through the things she wanted to keep and had decided to store the rest safely up here. Jeff had considered renting out Chloe's room to a lodger after she moved out to Oxford, and Connie's things were moved into the attic. The lodger never appeared, and Chloe always had the room to herself when she came back for the holidays. But Connie's old stuff also remained up here, out of sight.

Mark shone the light from his phone, and Chloe went through the garments carefully. At the bottom, her hand scraped across something hard. She thought it was a box, but the outline was smoother, the margins softer. She pulled it out. It was a brown leather notebook. Inside, the faded yellow paper bore Connie's neat, small writing that Chloe had seen in the past, on birthday and Christmas cards.

She stared at the pages. Was this a diary her mother kept? How had Chloe missed this? She closed the notebook slowly and clutched it tight. With her free hand, she rummaged around the rest of the box. She found another small book, like a telephone lister, with some photos inside. This book was strapped together with some rubber bands.

She unwrapped the rubber bands holding the book together and extricated the photos. Her father had told her he might have packed away some stuff, including photos, in the attic and hadn't said much more. She got the impression that, for him, some memories were best left hidden, and Jeff didn't want to face them. She didn't blame him. She knew about her mother's mental health issues, how she'd left one day and never returned. It had broken her father. He had raised Chloe as a single parent. Angela didn't come into their lives till Chloe was six years old. Perhaps there was more in these old boxes than she had bargained for, Chloe thought.

The photos were in colour and printed out on glossy paper. But the colours had faded. Chloe saw herself on her mother's lap. The others were of Connie with her friends. Chloe took the two notebooks and searched the rest of the box. She decided to take it downstairs, so Mark carefully carried it down.

Chloe lay on her bed, while Mark did some work on his laptop. She went through the photos. True, the photos she had already were much better than these. But she had never seen her mother's friends. She didn't recognise any of them, even allowing for the passage of time. One photo made her pause. It was a man, seated in the driver's seat of a car. He was looking at the camera and smiling. But the smile was cold and perfunctory, and his eyes were flat, dead. He had dark brown hair, a nose that was small and flat, and thin lips that stretched over a wide mouth. Chloe didn't like the look in the man's eyes. She wondered if he was one of Jeff's friends. But why would his photo be in Connie's stuff?

She put the photo to one side, not sure if she should ask her dad about it. She opened the diary. The journals were dated from January 2006.

I can't sleep. The voices keep coming back. That woman with that weird accent – is she Russian? I don't know. It hurts my ears. She's always criticising. I'm a bad mother because I fell asleep in the afternoon. Chloe woke me up with her crying. But I fed and cleaned her right away, didn't I? Chloe's happy, nothing's wrong with her.

With a sinking heart, Chloe carried on reading. Page after page described Connie's fragile state of mind. She kept hearing two women who talked about her. They also came into the house, according to Connie. They went through her desk drawers and looked inside her purse. Maybe they even looked inside the diary.

I told Jeff, and he took me to the doctor's. I don't want to start the medicines again. Last time, I put on so much weight. Jeff didn't like me anymore. Now he wants me to start the medicines again?

Chloe brushed away tears as she read the difficult pages. There was a blank for several weeks, then the journal picked up again in March 2006.

I saw him again today. There's something about him. He makes me feel like a woman. Jeff barely touches me anymore. He thinks I'm sick. Steven doesn't think so. He knows about the voices. He tells me they can be real, if I let them. He says I can't believe them. He's right. Oh Steven. I wish I could spend more time with you.

Chloe took a photo of the page with her phone. She scrolled through, reading the entries that had Steven in it.

Last night was so delicious. I put Chloe to bed and took some of Steven's medicine. I slept like a log. For the first time I felt refreshed.

But the tone changed a few weeks later. Connie's previous paranoia and anxiety screamed from the page.

Why won't these bitches leave me alone? I just need some rest! I can't even look after Chloe when I'm like this. And where's Steven? I need some medicine and he's not answering my calls.

Chloe picked up the photo of the man in the car. His strange, dead cold eyes stared back through the photo, as if he was looking directly at her. It made her shiver.

Was this the man called Steven?

In the last page of the diary entry, on 7 June 2006, Chloe got a clue.

I could meet Steven. He once said we could drive down to Iffley, where his mother lives. I'm not sure how far I want to take this. I know I want to see him for the medicine, but is that right? What should I do? I need to look after Chloe, nothing else is important.

So, this man called Steven lived in Iffley. That gave Chloe an idea. She didn't know who he was, but she now knew he was important in her mother's life. And, probably, in her disappearance.

SIXTEEN

Detective Constable Nish Bhatt stepped onto the sticky floor of Cargo nightclub, his senses instantly assaulted by the lingering stench of spilled alcohol and disinfectant. The place was empty now, the silence a contrast to what he imagined it must be like when packed with students – bodies grinding, music pounding, bass vibrating through the walls. Now, in the daylight, it felt bare, exposed.

Kristy Young was beside him, her coat still buttoned, eyes scanning the dimly lit interior. They made their way to the bar, where a man in his late forties, with slicked-back hair and the tired, wary expression of someone who'd seen too much, was polishing glasses.

Nish pulled out his warrant card, and showed it to the man. "Detective Constable Bhatt of Thames Valley Police. This is DC Young. We need to speak to your manager."

The bartender's face didn't flicker, but Nish caught the slight tightening of his fingers around the glass. "What's this about?"

"We need to ask about a woman who attended the premises.

The bartender exhaled sharply, then set the glass down. "Wait here."

He disappeared through a door behind the bar, and Nish turned to Kristy. She was checking out the ceiling, and pointed to the CCTV cameras placed prominently.

A few moments later, a man emerged. Late fifties, solid build, wearing a crisp black shirt and dark blue suit. His face was lined and worn, but his blue eyes were sharp, calculating.

"I'm Richard Farnham," he said. "I manage Cargo. What can I do for you?"

Nish introduced himself and Kristy again. He took out his phone, pulled up the photo of Chloe Pierson, and held it up. You remember her?"

Farnham glanced at the photo. "I don't keep track of every customer who walks through my doors."

"She was a regular," Kristy said. "Your staff would've known her. She was here Thursday and Saturday most weeks."

Farnham's jaw tightened, just for a moment. "Maybe. I don't remember. Look, whatever happened to this woman, I'm sorry. But it didn't happen here."

"Yes," Nish said slowly, not liking the manager's reluctance to cooperate. "But she did attend this place, with her friends. All we want is some information. Can we speak to your staff?"

Mr Farnham hesitated. "Will this be out in the papers? I can't afford to have the name of the club out in the papers, if you know what I mean. It's bad for business."

"No," Nish said. "The media has not been alerted, and even if they were, your club will not be mentioned. That's part of the investigation, and it's confidential."

Farnham still looked undecided. His eyes flicked between Nish and Kristy, as if trying to decide if he could trust them.

Kristy let out a quiet sigh. "We can get a warrant and come back later. Or you can cooperate now and save us all the paperwork."

Farnham folded his arms. "I run a legitimate business. If you're asking me whether there was trouble that night, the answer's no. If you're asking whether we've got CCTV, the answer's yes. But I need to know what exactly you're looking for."

"Anyone Chloe Pierson was with," Nish said. "Her behaviour. Anything unusual."

Farnham hesitated, then nodded. "Fine. Follow me."

They walked past the bar and through a side door into the staff corridor, past posters warning against drugs and aggressive behaviour. The CCTV room was cramped, a small desk covered in monitors, the air thick with the smell of stale coffee. A security guard, a tall Afro Caribbean man with a shaved head, was hunched over the screen.

"This is Marcus," Farnham said. "He's one of our bouncers. He was on duty last night."

Marcus turned, giving the detectives a slow, assessing look, then glancing at his boss. "What's this about?"

Nish told him, and then showed him Chloe's photo. Marcus squinted at the photo, and then he frowned, slowly rubbing his chin.

Nish asked, "You saw her?"

Marcus exhaled through his nose. "Yeah. I remember her from last night. Seen her before as well, to be honest. She was here with her mates like usual, but she left in a hurry. Something spooked her."

"What do you mean, 'spooked her'?" Kristy asked, leaning forward.

"She ran out. Almost tripped over her own feet. Looked over her shoulder like someone was chasing her."

Nish frowned. "Did anyone follow her?"

Marcus shook his head. "Not that I saw. She bolted. Didn't see where she went."

"Who was she with?" Kristy pressed.

"Same crowd as usual. Blonde girl, I think, and some bloke. Tall, dark hair. I've seen him with her before. Black kid."

"You have footage?" Nish asked.

Marcus nodded and sat down at his desk. Nish and Kristy pulled up chairs. Mr Farnham stood behind them, watching. Marcus rewound the tapes. The grainy colour screen flickered, showing a crowd of people at the bar. Marcus changed screens, and now they saw the view from a camera above the entrance corridor. A few people walked past, and Marcus slowed the footage. They saw Chloe, walking with a blonde.

"Zoom in," Nish said. Marcus did so, and Kristy leaned forward. "That's Jemima, isn't it?"

"Yes," Nish said slowly. Nish and Kristy exchanged a glance. Jemima was lying when she said she wasn't at the nightclub.

Then the next clip made Nish lean in closer. Chloe was in an argument with an Afro Caribbean man. Her hands were moving in the air, and she seemed agitated.

"Is that Mark?" Kristy asked.

"I think so," Nish said. "Looks similar to the photo on his student ID."

Then Mark gripped her wrist. She tried to yank herself free, but he pulled her back, speaking rapidly into her ear. Her face twisted – anger, fear, desperation. Then, with one final wrench, she broke free and shoved him back. Mark stumbled, then straightened, his face cold, watching her as she ran out of the club. Marcus changed angles on the screen, and he zoomed in on Chloe's face as she ran out. The panic was clearly written on her features.

"This Mark," Nish said. "He's a regular?"

Marcus hesitated, then nodded. "Yeah. I've seen him before, with that woman." He pointed at the image of Chloe.

Nish clenched his jaw. This fit with what they were starting to piece together – Chloe had been in something deeper than just student parties and casual drug dealing. And whatever it was, Mark had been involved.

Kristy exhaled, rubbing her temple. "We need this footage."

Farnham nodded. "I'll get you a copy on a memory stick."

Before they left the office, Nish glanced back at the screen, at Chloe's stressed face frozen in time. She had been afraid of something. And that something had killed her.

"Back to the station?" Kristy asked.

Nish nodded. "Yeah. The guv will be interested to know that Jemima's been lying."

SEVENTEEN

Monty was on the phone to Turnham High School. He put the phone down and pursed his lips together, a thoughtful expression on his face.

"Any news?" Nikki asked.

"Yes." Monty sighed. "I asked the headmaster about Mark. He said Mark was part of a gang at the school. They supplied other students with drugs and had initiation rites."

"Such as?" Nikki raised her eyebrows. "Turnham High School is well-regarded, right? I didn't realise this kind of thing would be happening there."

"Happens in every college, especially with boys, I think. And this was a boys-only boarding school, like Eton or Harrow. Anyway, the headmaster was sketchy on the details, maybe to protect the college's reputation. The gang was like a secret society, and to become a member you had to perform certain, shall we say, acts – like killing a farmer's pig, pouring the blood over a 'normal' student's head, that sort of thing. They were quite notorious."

Nikki shook her head. She had also looked at the college's prospectus. "Forty grand a year, and this is what the boys get up to. Not surprising, I guess. Some of these kids have all the money in the world, don't they? They come from privileged backgrounds."

"But not Mark." Monty raised a hand. "He was completely the opposite. He had no money, and he was also a Black boy in a predominantly white school. That was probably the reason why he tried so hard to fit in. He became notorious, and the others accepted him for that. It became his trademark, so to speak. And despite everything, he was good academically, which is how he got into Oxford."

"He's an interesting character, that's for sure."

Monty steepled his fingers in front of his face, then slid them under his chin. His strong jawline and full lips became prominent. Nikki watched as he became lost in thought.

"Mark and Chloe went into Cowley, but we lost them after that, which is a shame," Monty said. Traffic are now looking for Mark using facial recognition software, aren't they?"

"Yes, but it's a needle in a haystack. Hopefully, they come up with something soon."

The office door opened and Nish and Kristy came in. Nish told Nikki about their visit to Cargo, while Kristy loaded the CCTV footage from the nightclub. They gathered around Kristy's chair to look at the screen.

Nikki tapped her lower lip when Jemima's face became visible. Kristy was able to pick the girls up as they went inside the main dance floor, and they saw them meeting up with two other women. Kristy zoomed in again, and Nikki identified Fiona.

At the end of the footage, Nikki said, "All the more important now to find Mark. But I want to speak to Jemima and Fiona again." She addressed Nish. "You two – go through all the footage. Focus on Mark and see if he speaks to anyone else. Get back to the Cargo security staff if you need to follow up any leads."

"On it, guv," Nish said.

Nikki and Monty went outside. As they walked down the car park, Nikki thought of the note in Chloe's coat pocket.

Ask DI Nikki Gill what happened.

It had to be an insider in the police force. What could be another explanation? Someone was keeping an eye on her, tracking her career? That was laughable paranoia. Or was it?

Nikki had caught her fair share of psychopaths and dangerous, obsessive men. They were all in prison, but what if one of them had a contact outside?

But surely the chances of that happening were slim to non-existent.

"Penny for your thoughts," Monty said. Nikki realised she was standing there, head bowed as she thought. Monty came closer.

"You alright?"

"Yes, it's just that note in Chloe's pocket. Who could it be?"

Monty's tone was measured, like his warm voice. "We can take everyone who had contact with the body to one side and ask them. The police staff, and the groundsman who found her. Shall we do that?"

"Was it one of them?" Nikki wished she didn't sound so desperate.

"Well..." Monty sat down again. "Did someone put the note in her pocket before she fell from the wall? That could mean at any point in the evening – when she was in the nightclub, for example."

"Or earlier when she was with Mark."

"Exactly. So the actual pool of suspects is wider." Monty shrugged. "I know that doesn't help you much. But we could start with the people we know had contact with Chloe, both before and immediately after death."

Nikki nodded. She needed to do something, the anxiety was

creeping inside her. If this was someone's idea of a prank, it wasn't funny. "Yes, I guess we do that. Thanks." She gave Monty a wan, tired smile. "Let's go."

* * *

The man was waiting at the police station. He was in his car, an old van that had seen better days. He saw Nikki Gill emerge, with the tall Indian Inspector next to her. He couldn't remember his name. The man focused his attention on Nikki. The way she moved, her expressions, reminded her of someone he once knew.

He watched as the couple walked slowly down the pavement, engrossed in conversation. He found their body language interesting. The man was leaning forward, and she wasn't exactly keeping her distance. Were they more than colleagues? He felt a stab of jealousy. Nikki wasn't exactly his type. He liked them younger than her. He wanted them to be weak and vulnerable, so tortured by their pain they would willingly accept the release he gave them.

No, it wasn't jealousy. It was possessiveness. Nikki was like family, after all. He needed to look after her. He smiled. That note he had deftly tucked into Chloe's pocket was a masterstroke. Not his usual style, but an inspirational move. He knew Nikki had found the note. He could see it in her troubled face. Whom it came from and why would be eating away at her inside.

She would find out, but the time hadn't arrived yet. The old man smiled like a cunning wolf. He had far better plans in store for Nikki Gill.

EIGHTEEN

Eighteen years ago

Connie felt cold, clammy and restless. Her nose was running, sweat pouring down her forehead.

She held Chloe's hand as they walked slowly down the road. Chloe tugged on her hand when she saw a dog. Connie pulled Chloe away, a little harder than she had intended. Chloe cried, and Connie regretted it immediately. The woman walking the dog gave her a funny look. Ashamed, Connie knelt and cuddled Chloe. She picked her up and kissed her on the cheek. She gave Chloe a sweet, which improved the little one's mood considerably. Connie put her down again, then blew her nose. She felt horrible. She had spent the morning in the bathroom, vomiting. She was on edge, her heart rate supersonic. It was like this when the medicine wore off. She hadn't been to him for a few days because she was trying to see less of him. She knew she was getting hooked on the medicine. When she didn't have it, she wanted it. Connie wasn't a fool. She knew she was now a drug addict. Her head sank to her chest, and shame collided with regret in her heart. She should have gone to the doctor's, like Jeffrey had told her to. She should have got the tablets and seen the psychiatrist.

This was wrong. This feeling of walking a tightrope, being constantly on edge. The voices came and went and got worse when she was tired or stressed. Chloe was a good baby, bless her. The toddler was happy and active; she had the usual accidents in the playground, falling over. Once, she fell backwards at home and hit her head on the stairs. Connie was in the kitchen, and she came running. There was some blood and she'd rushed Chloe to the hospital. That had been scary, but luckily it didn't happen again. Connie was ashamed that as she waited in the emergency room with Chloe, her mind kept returning to when she would get her next fix. More than shame, she felt rotten to the core. Wasted and hollowed out inside. No, she couldn't do this anymore.

She guided Chloe down the two blocks to the nursery. They moved along slowly, and – normally – she enjoyed her walks with Chloe. But today was different. She had to make up her mind, and the longer she waited, the deeper she slipped into the mire. The sinking sands of addiction were now coming up to her neck, and soon she would be submerged completely.

Jeffrey knew something was up, and he asked her why she was always either tired or anxious, and sleeping in the daytime. When he came back from work, she was often passed out on the couch, and Connie still needed to apologise to the nursery staff who filled her phone with messages. Connie had apologised to them profusely, but she knew they were also suspicious something was wrong with her. They had called in Jeffrey, and he had had to explain about her mental health. It was time she sorted herself out.

The sun was bright, but it was cold. They got to the nursery, and Connie hugged and kissed Chloe, who was then taken inside by one of the carers. One year ago, Chloe cried all the time when she went to nursery, and it broke Connie's heart. Now, she smiled as she went inside without even looking back. Chloe was eager to play with her new friends.

Her little girl was the only slice of sunlight in Connie's dark life. As she watched Chloe go inside, Connie knew she had to do this for her daughter. She had to clean herself up.

She went to see her doctor. Dr Jaya Patel, her GP, had a sympathetic look on her face as Connie explained her situation. She knew Connie well, and none of it was new to her. Connie left out the details of her addiction. She said she was taking too many sleeping pills, which she was getting from a friend. The lie seemed to work, as Dr Patel was concerned.

"Sleeping pills can be very addictive. Take diazepam, for example. If you try to stop them suddenly, they can give you seizures. That can be life-threatening."

Connie nodded in silence, not giving anything away. Dr Patel asked, "Where are you getting the pills from?"

"A friend who came from Germany," Connie lied. "But that's not important. I want to start on the medications again. Can you please prescribe them?"

Dr Patel looked into her notes and gave Connie the medications the psychiatrist had prescribed six months ago: a combination of antidepressants and antipsychotics.

"You start on a low dose, and after one week increase it. Slowly the dose increases over one month. You won't see any positive effects for about a month, but you need to persevere." Dr Patel's kind face broke into an encouraging smile. "You want to do this, don't you?"

Connie's fists were tightly clenched in her lap. "Yes, I do."

She took the medication, went home, and started taking it

immediately. But she was still restless. Her bowels were loose, and nausea rose up in her throat. She knew that she needed to see him for just one last fix. And it would be the very last. She had read up about addiction online. The articles said there was no such thing as the last fix because there was always one more. She had to go cold turkey, and she had to do it now. The last three nights, she hadn't slept. She sweated continuously, and her teeth chattered as she shivered with cold, even while the heating was on.

She paced the kitchen, then went outside into the garden. Sunlight fell on the back fence, and she shivered in the cold, dragging her cardigan tightly around her. There was a sharp pain behind her eyes, and her limbs felt heavy, dragging her down. She was also restless, despite the constant ache in her legs. It was like moving through treacle, a constant fog of pain and sickness. She had to distract herself somehow. She turned the TV on, but that didn't work. She heard a phone beep and snatched it up. It was one of her friends, wanting to meet up for coffee. Connie hadn't seen any of her friends for days. She didn't want them to suspect anything and report back to Jeffrey. Her landline started to ring. Connie was surprised, as in the daytime that phone didn't normally ring. Hesitantly, she picked it up.

"Hello?"

The heavy male voice on the other end was unmistakable. "Why are you avoiding me?"

Connie trembled, a numbness spreading into her limbs. "How did you get this number?"

"Just answer my question. Why?"

"I don't want to do this anymore. It was a mistake. I want you to leave me alone."

He was silent for a while. "Has your husband found out?"

"What..." Connie started. "No. It doesn't matter. This is about me. I don't want to do this anymore. I've been to see the doctor. I've started taking the tablets again."

"You know that doesn't work. That's how we found each other. Those tablets will mess up your mind, and you'll become dependent on them."

"And I'm not dependent on this shit that you're injecting me with? You know how horrible it is? I'd much rather be on the tablets."

She heard his heavy breathing and the soft buzz of static. When he spoke, his words were gentler. "I'm sorry. I know it's not been easy for you. It's not about the medicine. It's about us. I want to see you get well and be happy. I want us to be together."

Connie's mind was going round in circles. He knew where she lived and could contact her any time. She didn't like that at all. But she had to let him down gently.

"I don't want to be with you anymore," she said, mustering up all the courage she had. "I'm sorry. It's over."

His breathing became faster, and she could tell he was getting angry. He had never lost his temper with her, but she knew there was always an undercurrent of violence. She had seen him in an argument with another man before. He had hit the man, one of his drug dealers, and knocked him out cold. She knew he could be dangerous.

"You're not thinking straight," he said. "You need the medicine. Why don't you come to the park, and we could go for a ride?"

"You're not listening to me," Connie said. "I feel terrible. I don't want to do this anymore. And I don't want to see you anymore."

Silence again. Then he spoke in an eerie, calm voice, his

words chilling her heart. "I know where Chloe goes to nursery. I can see her playing inside, through the fence."

Connie couldn't speak. Fear had driven nails through her tongue, her mind frozen.

He spoke softly. "Do you want to see your daughter again?"

"You wouldn't dare..." she breathed finally. "Go anywhere near my daughter, and I'll make you pay."

"It doesn't have to be like this, Connie. I just want us to be together."

"Why are you threatening me and my daughter if you want us to be together?"

"I'm sorry. I got angry, that's all. I thought I was able to give you some relief from the voices, from all that pain you had to endure. That's worth fighting for, isn't it?"

"No," she said firmly. "That's just an illusion. The reality comes back a hundred times worse. I don't even know what's real or fake anymore. Your medicine is wrecking my life."

His voice hardened, and his breathing grew faster again. "This will not end well for you. I want to see you again. Otherwise, I know where Chloe is right now. I also know where your mother lives, in Swindon."

Connie's heart was hammering against her chest, and she thought she would pass out. "What... How do you...?"

"Catherine McLauchlan? That's your mother, isn't it? Yes, I know she lives in Seaview Avenue, in Swindon. I know a lot about you. See, we're meant to be together. I want us to bring our families close together. You, me, and Chloe can live in the same house one day."

"Stay away from me. Stay away from my daughter. I'll tell the police about you. I know your car's registration number."

"If you want to play that game, fair enough. But Chloe will be long gone, and so will your mother, before the police know anything. Is this how you want to play it?"

Connie slumped down on the floor. She gripped her forehead. She was panicked, confused, but she had to get a grip. "What do you want?"

"I want you to see me. Tonight, at the usual place. If you don't, Chloe disappears."

With a click, the line went dead.

NINETEEN

All of the Oxford colleges were beautiful, and each one had its unique charm. But to Nikki's mind, All Souls College was particularly special. They stood outside the north quadrangle, which faced Radcliffe Square. Students and pedestrians milled about on the ancient cobblestone path that circled around the huge dome of the Radcliffe Observatory in front of the college.

"Shall we go inside?" Monty asked.

Nikki nodded, and they went through a long, stone entrance that opened up into the green quadrangle. It was here that All Souls' similarity with other Oxford colleges ended. It was more of a cathedral than a college. The long Gothic spires were visionary, with intricate carvings on them. They rose high into the air, and the long stained-glass window of the front facade glinted in the sunlight. Nikki always felt she was transported to another world when she stepped inside All Souls College.

Nikki and Monty came upon a narrow, curved stone staircase that led up to the Fellows' Passage, and their footsteps echoed against the cloistered walls as they walked up to the first floor. The hallway here was suddenly wide and spacious, with a balcony overlooking the quadrangle and, on the left, the large rooms reserved for the Fellows. All Souls College was unique because it didn't have any undergraduates, only academics. The professors here taught students at most of the colleges.

"It's number seven," Monty said, remembering what the porters had told them. Nikki looked at her watch. It was just past three p.m., and the tutorial was supposed to have finished five minutes ago. She hoped they wouldn't have to wait long; she needed to get back to the station.

She whispered to Monty, "What if she's not here?"

"She will be," Monty replied. "Final year students don't miss tutorials."

"You're very confident for someone who's not studied here."

Monty rolled his eyes. "Not this again. I've been in more investigations in the colleges than you have." He grinned at her and lowered his face close to hers. "Just because you're from Oxford doesn't mean you know everything about it."

"You're all talk sometimes, you know that?" She prodded him on the arm. She stared at the light dancing in his eyes and the smooth brown contours of his handsome face. That craggy jawline and the high cheekbones. She wanted to touch his face, slide her fingers down his beard. Then she blinked and lowered her eyes to the floor.

Monty straightened, and when she looked up at him, he was staring ahead. She gave him a smile, and he reciprocated.

The door behind them opened, and Jemima stepped out. She halted in her tracks, clutching the books she carried close to her chest. The colour drained from her face, and the light makeup couldn't hide the dark shadows under her eyes.

"Hi, Jemima." Nikki stepped forward. "We just want to ask you a few more questions about Chloe. I hope you don't mind."

Jemima, flustered, shut the door behind her. Her teeth were clenched, and she folded her arms across her chest, balancing her books against herself.

"What did you want to talk about?" she asked in a low, hesitant voice.

"Shall we sit down somewhere?" Nikki said lightly. "There's a café outside, on the High Street, and I can buy you a drink."

Jemima's eyes flicked to Monty, who stood silently behind Nikki. She was reluctant, and the conflict on her face was clear. But eventually, she nodded.

Once they'd sat down at the back of the quiet café and placed their order, Nikki said, "I know that Chloe's death is a huge shock. When I saw you in your room, we didn't have a proper conversation, did we? There are things about Chloe that we need to discuss."

In Jemima's pale face, a new wariness appeared. Nikki decided to be open with her.

"We've spoken to Chloe's other friends. We know she took ecstasy and went out clubbing."

Jemima blinked, then nodded in silence.

Nikki said, "This does not affect your place as a student at the college. Your tutors will never know, and anything you tell us is confidential."

"You don't think it was an accident, then?"

Monty narrowed his eyes and shot Nikki a look. A niggling suspicion tugged at the back of Nikki's mind.

"We're keeping our minds open at this point in time," Nikki said, drawing Jemima's attention back to her. "What do you think happened?"

"I don't know, I've told you that already."

"Were you on the college grounds late last night? Students were heard around one or two a.m."

Jemima looked down at her hands. She moved them from the table, and Nikki could tell they were twisting in her lap. The fact that she was being evasive bothered Nikki. She decided to come clean.

"Jemima, we know you went to Cargo last night with Chloe."

Jemima's head shot up, and she stared at Nikki with shocked eyes.

"We have you and Chloe on CCTV, at Cargo. Why did you lie to us?"

Jemima's head lowered, then moved from side to side. "I don't know," she said in a small voice. "I was scared. I'm sorry." She touched her forehead.

Nikki watched her, wondering if she was being honest. Her instincts told her Jemima wasn't dangerous. Her emotions seemed genuine, and Nikki didn't think she was acting. But she had to keep an open mind.

Jemima's eyes flickered down to her lap, where her hands twisted. "Talk to us, Jemima," Nikki said in a soft, reassuring voice. "You're not in any danger. Help us find out what happened to Chloe."

Jemima nodded once, still looking down. Then slowly, she raised her head.

"We went out to Cargo, the nightclub near the station. Chloe was there, but she was acting weird. Then she left. I don't know where she went. Mark was also there, in case you want to know."

Jemima looked up and held Nikki's gaze. "I'm not sure, but I think Mark and Chloe had an argument. Chloe didn't seem happy."

"How was she acting weird?" Monty asked.

"Like paranoid. She thought someone in the club was watching her. An old man with a beard."

"Old, bearded man? In a nightclub?"

"That's what she said." Jemima shrugged.

"Chloe didn't say goodbye before she left? But you went out together, right?"

"No. She went out for dinner earlier. She didn't say with

who. I assumed it was with Mark, but when I asked him at the nightclub, he denied it."

Nikki frowned, mirroring the expression on Monty's face.

"Do you know if Chloe went to Iffley that night?"

Jemima frowned. "Iffley? No, I don't think so. Well, she didn't say anything."

"Has she been to Iffley in the past?"

"She mentioned it once, yes. She had met someone who knew her mother."

"Did she tell you who this man was? Did she describe him?"

"Well, he was old, given he was her mother's friend. She said that." Jemima stopped and stared at Nikki, then at Monty. "You don't think... he was the old guy Chloe was seeing around? Did he follow her?"

Nikki shook her head slightly. "We don't know. But we have to consider it."

The drinks arrived, and Jemima took a long sip of her tea. With the confession, a load seemed to have dropped from her shoulders. She looked relieved.

Nikki asked, "Do you know when Chloe went to Iffley?"

"No, sorry."

Nikki watched her for a few seconds, then decided to move on.

"Tell me what happened at the nightclub."

"I was at the nightclub with Chloe, Mark, Fiona and a few of Fiona's friends from other colleges. They were all members of TITS. We got back to the college around one in the morning, but I wasn't sure of the time. Yes, we did go out into the grounds, even though it's not allowed."

Her eyes flicked up to Nikki, and the corners of her lips twitched. "But we do it all the time. The tutors and porters usually don't find out." Her face clouded over, and her lips parted. Her eyes lost their focus.

"Was Mark there?"

"No. I assumed he left the nightclub before us."

"In the college grounds, who else was out there with you?"

"Fiona, Bridget and Kelly. We stayed out for a smoke. Fiona walked off on her own for a while."

"Did you see Chloe there?"

Jemima frowned. "No, I didn't. Was she there?"

"Yes. What time did you get back? Approximately?"

"It wasn't that late. Before one a.m. About quarter to one, I think."

Nikki nodded. "Chloe came back about fifteen minutes before you did. We saw her on CCTV."

Jemima narrowed her eyes, thinking.

"What happened after you got back?" Nikki pressed.

"We had a smoke, then went upstairs."

"What about Fiona?"

Jemima blinked a few times. "Sorry, I can't recall."

"So Fiona could've stayed on the grounds, with Chloe?" Nikki asked, glancing at Monty. He nodded approvingly.

"I don't know," Jemima said. She narrowed her eyes, trying to think. "Sorry, I should know that, I guess."

Monty tapped Jemima's arm and she turned to him. "Don't worry. How was Chloe's relationship with Fiona?"

A shadow passed over Jemima's face, and Nikki caught it. Jemima was silent for a while.

"Go on," Nikki urged.

Jemima swallowed once before replying. "Fiona fancied Mark. They'd been seen together... I mean, I saw them once and told Chloe. She confronted Mark. He said nothing was going on between them, they were just friends. But from then on, she wasn't on good terms with Fiona."

Jemima was silent, and Nikki pressed her lips tightly together, thinking. Fiona had been at the club last night. She wondered if the girls had a fight, which could be bad, fuelled by alcohol.

Monty caught Nikki's attention and mouthed a word to her. Nikki understood.

"Do you know if Chloe was dealing drugs?"

Jemima looked up, her mouth open in disbelief. She didn't reply immediately. Then she shook her head. "No," she whispered.

"We found a stash in her room," Nikki said. "Please keep this confidential. She had enough cocaine and ecstasy pills to supply a lot of people. We're talking high-purity cocaine here, not something you'd get from a street dealer."

Jemima frowned, her lips parted. She swallowed and shut her mouth with effort. "I mean, we did drugs, but we had a supplier. I didn't know Chloe had a stash that big."

"Who was your supplier?"

Jemima looked up at her, their eyes locking. "It was one of Mark's friends."

Nikki narrowed her eyes. "Who?"

"We never knew. I don't know if Chloe did. But Mark always seemed to have a ready supply of the stuff."

Nikki looked at Monty. His jaws were stiff, and she knew from the steely determination in his eyes that finding Mark was now even more of a priority.

TWENTY

Eight weeks ago

Of all the charming riverine villages that surrounded Oxford, Iffley was one of the most picturesque.

From the photos in her mum's diary, Chloe had got the man's car's registration number. It had taken some digging around, but luckily for her records at the DVLA were digitised from April 2005. She had to request permission to check the vehicle's details, as it had expired, and the car's whereabouts were unknown. Which meant, the man at the other end of the line told her, it was in a scrap yard, and had probably been sold for steel already.

However, the helpful man told Chloe she had to fill in a form called a V888. As long as she had a valid reason, she could get the names of all the previous owners of the vehicle. Chloe put in the reason as looking for her mother's missing partner, and the request was fulfilled.

From there, she got the 2006 owner's full name and registered address. It had been registered under a woman's name with the same last name as him, which Chloe thought must be his mother, or wife. From the woman's name, she got the address in Iffley.

The house was tucked away in a charming little corner close to the High Street and Iffley Lock on the Thames. The market was on today. It was Saturday, and according to the sign, the market was on twice a month. Farmers had set up stalls, selling all kinds of meat and vegetables. Other shops, selling cake, pies, Indian and Japanese food, were also out in force. Chloe had no idea Iffley market was this big. She wandered around for a few minutes, as she had to walk through the market.

Her heart beat faster as she got to the street in question. It was a turning from the main road, that sloped down to the river. She had left the sound and smell of the market behind her now, and it was quiet.

Chloe walked down the street, watching the pretty, stone-walled houses, typical of the Cotswolds. Green ivy crept along several walls, and potted plants rested on windowsills. She stopped a few doors away from number forty-two, on the opposite side.

A woman came out with a child in a pram from the house next to her. She stopped in front of Chloe and looked at her inquisitively.

"Hi." Chloe smiled. "I'm a student at New College, Oxford, and we're doing a survey on the residents of Iffley. It's for my Economics degree. We're creating a register of what people do, their ages, so on. It's all anonymised data. Nothing that can identify anyone. I spoke to Miss Charlesworth, next door to you, yesterday."

Chloe showed her student ID badge and put on her best smile. Her heart was thumping loudly. The woman examined her ID then looked back at her.

She shrugged, the cautious expression still remaining on her face. "Sure. What would you like to know?"

"Number forty-two," Chloe pointed at the house opposite. The woman turned to look. "Do you know who lives there? I've knocked on two separate days, but I didn't get a response."

That was a lie, like her previous project. But she had to try something. The man called Steven had been an enigma so far. She couldn't find him.

"Oh yes. An old lady lived there. Mrs Pugh. She died recently, and her son moved in."

Chloe's breathing kicked up a notch. "Have you seen her son?"

"A couple of times. Maybe if you leave a note through the door, he can get back to you?"

"Sure." Chloe hoped she had an easy smile on her face. "What does he look like? I mean, is he old, young..."

The woman stared at her, and Chloe wondered if she'd gone too far. Then the woman spoke casually. "He's elderly himself. Mrs Pugh had lived here all her life. She was a hundred years old. I remember one of the neighbours saying she got a letter from the king."

The son was Steven, Chloe knew. She desperately wanted to ask more questions about his appearance, but decided against it.

"Thank you." She smiled. "You've been very helpful. Is it okay if I knock on your door sometime later next week? I'm still working through the other houses."

"Alright." The woman gave Chloe a tight smile, and then walked away with her pram. Chloe walked down the street, and past number forty-two. There was an alley between the terraced houses that led to the next street. She slipped into the alley, and watched the house.

Her heart jumped when she saw a shadow pass in front of the upstairs window. She watched with bated breath as a tall, old man with white hair and stooped shoulders emerged from the house. He locked the door, and then walked down the street, his gait firm and surprisingly quick. A heavy cloth bag bulged at his side.

TWENTY-ONE

Eight weeks ago

Chloe came out of the alley and followed the man, keeping a safe distance. At the end of the road, he turned left, towards the river and the market. She quickened her pace, afraid of losing him. She caught up as they got closer to the market, and the crowds got thicker. The man slipped behind a row of stalls.

Chloe walked around the main market path, in front of the stalls. The man had his own stall, which surprised her. It was a charity for elderly people. The stall was already set up, filled with trays of chocolates and cakes. Chloe realised he must have been at this the whole morning and had just popped to his house to get the bag.

Her stomach rumbled; the cakes looked good. She'd only had a yogurt for breakfast. Chloe felt a strange sensation waft through her as she stared at him. Was this the man her mother had been to see, when she'd gone out and never returned? The man with whom she was having an affair?

And what about the medicine he had given Connie?

Too many questions. Steeling herself, Chloe stepped forward. He looked up as she approached.

Yes, he was the same man as in that photo. Sitting in the car, staring out at the person taking the photo. Steven. Age had mellowed his eyes, and his face had lost the hard angles. His cheeks had sagged, and his eyebrows were bushy. The hair was thinning at the top. But he had a strength in his shoulder and arms, was still thick set across the chest.

"Hello." He smiled, the crow's feet at the corners of his eyes crinkling. But there was a wariness in his blue eyes.

"Are you Steven Pugh?" Chloe asked.

He blinked a few times, and leaned forward, as if he hadn't heard her question. "I beg your pardon?"

Chloe stepped closer to the table. She repeated her question. Steven straightened, and the careful appraisal remained in his eyes. Then he nodded.

"Who wants to know?" He smiled, to dispel the awkwardness.

"I'm Chloe Pierson. You knew my mother. Constance. Connie Pierson?"

Steven's lips parted, and a shadow passed over his face. He was searching for an answer. Chloe suspected he remembered Connie.

"Sorry. Who did you say?"

"Connie Pierson. She lived in Wolvercote, back in 2006. She knew you. Do you remember her?"

Steven blinked a few times. He stood straighter and stroked his beard.

Chloe wasn't letting him get away that easily. She took the photo out from her satchel bag and held it up.

"That's you in the car, isn't it?"

Steven leaned forward, and his eyebrows lifted. He looked at Chloe with a new light in his eyes.

"My gosh, yes. That's my old car, and me, alright." He

stroked his beard again, and a look of wonder swam across his face. "Gosh, that takes me back a long time. Connie, yes, I knew her. She was a friend of a friend. Didn't know her that well, mind. How is she? Did you say you're her daughter?"

"Yes, I am." Chloe got the distinct impression Steven was trying to hide the truth. His expression had veered from carefully disguised shock to fake friendliness. She suspected he knew very well what happened to her mother.

"When did you last see Connie?"

Steven shook his head once, the tight smile slipping from his face. His flat blue eyes were now cold and steely – the same look he had in that old photo.

"A long time ago, like I said." He shrugged.

"You didn't stay in touch with her?"

"No. We sort of drifted apart, I guess. Can I ask what this is about?"

"So you don't know what happened to her?"

Steven frowned. "From your questions, it seems something bad happened to her. Is that correct?"

"Yes. She went missing and was never found."

The surprise on Steven's face looked genuine. Or he was a very good actor. "Really? But... she had a family. Husband and daughter." That expansive, wonderous look appeared on his face again. "That daughter is you." His frowned again. "You said she was never found. I'm sure her husband notified the police, right?"

"Yes." Chloe watched him for a while. He held her gaze. "My mother knew you." Chloe wasn't about to disclose the presence of the diary. Not yet. "Did you have an affair with her?"

Steven looked surprised, then recovered. His jaws relaxed, and his shoulders dropped a touch.

"Yes," he said quietly. "We did. It didn't last long. We both knew it wouldn't go anywhere. We broke up after a few weeks."

Chloe stared at him, and this time Steven lowered his head. "I'm sorry. I didn't know about this. I moved out of Wolvercote, and went up north to work. I lost touch with my friends down here. That's why I didn't know, I guess."

When he looked up, Chloe saw a heaviness in his eyes she hadn't expected. He said, "When you live as long as I have, you count every day as a blessing. My poor mother passed away three months ago. That's when I moved down here. And to be honest, I was thinking about getting in touch with my friends again. I'm glad you came to see me." He smiled, and it was warmer, touching his eyes.

"How did you find me?"

"Not hard these days. I had your old car's registration number."

"You're a resourceful girl, aren't you? Your mother would've been proud." He angled his head and stroked his beard again. "Actually, I can see shades of Connie in you."

He wasn't getting off that easily, Chloe thought to herself. But she was feeling less uneasy as their conversation progressed. She felt genuine remorse from Steven.

"I want you to think carefully, please. As you can imagine, both my father and I want to find out what happened to Connie. Can you recall anything at all? She vanished shortly after she knew you. Did you plan to meet her anywhere, and she didn't turn up?"

"No," Steven said firmly. "In fact, she broke it off, not me. We didn't meet up anywhere after the summer of that year. 2006, did you say?"

Chloe nodded. "Did you know about my mother's mental health issues?"

"Yes. She spoke of it. She was troubled by it." Steven closed his eyes and took a deep breath. "She was beautiful, your mother was. A frail and tragic beauty. And I'm sorry I didn't do much to help her."

His face suffused with crimson, and to Chloe's surprise, tears budded in his eyes. He brushed them off with a meaty forearm and sniffed. He lifted the apron and dabbed at his eyes.

"I'm sorry for your loss. I really am. I can also see why you would be suspicious of me, as I knew Connie in her last days. But I didn't have anything to do with her disappearing. I..." He swallowed, and then his voice broke. "I thought I loved her, back then. That's why we had to end it."

Chloe was surprised by the turn of his feelings. He was cautious at first, but now he was full of regret. And she didn't think it was contrived.

"Thank you," she found herself saying. Still, her previous scepticism remained. Connie had disappeared the night she had written in her diary that she was going to visit Steven. No one had seen that diary entry till Chloe found it last week.

"Seventh June 2006," Chloe said. "That was the last day my mum was seen. She was going to see you."

"But I didn't know about it. Honest to God. Did she actually tell someone that? Then why haven't the police been in touch with me already?"

No, Chloe thought in silence. She didn't tell anyone. That's the whole point. Was Steven lying now?

She felt conflicted. Steven's remorse came off him in waves. It was markedly different to what she had expected.

"It's good to meet you." Steven wiped his eyes. "You remind me of her. Here, please have a seat. Or would you like to come to the house? I live just around the corner."

Chloe felt a little bad now, given how she had been snooping around. She nodded. "Sure, thank you. Do you still work, or are you retired?"

"I am retired. I used to be a gas engineer. Now I do some voluntary work for the university, to check their boilers." He smiled. "Keeps me occupied. And I'm a part of this charity. My mother was a donor, and I decided to do my bit."

He pulled up a chair. Chloe thanked him but remained standing. "So, you did not know where my mother was going that night she vanished? It seemed as if she was going to meet you."

"And who told you that?"

Chloe hesitated, then decided to tell him the truth. "She kept a diary. I read it there."

"And she wrote in the diary she was going to meet me?"

"She was planning to meet you," Chloe admitted. Connie didn't write she was definitely going to meet Steven.

"And I don't remember a plan like that, even allowing for all the time that's passed. I'm sorry. To be honest, if she had planned to meet me, and then didn't turn up, I would've remembered. I might even have got in touch with the police myself.

Chloe shrugged. "I guess so." She was mollified by Steven's responses, but the kernel of doubt remained in her mind. Connie didn't exactly write about Steven in glowing terms. But it also seemed Steven was genuine in his remorse.

Steven pulled out a tray from under the counter. This tray was small, the size of a dinner plate. It had small chocolates on it, and was covered in cellophane paper. Each chocolate had a distinctive red and black wrapper.

"Here, have some of these. They're my best-selling batch of chocolates."

Chloe hesitated. Steven took the cellophane off and pushed the tray towards her.

"Please, take some. In fact, take anything you want. No need to buy anything."

Chloe looked at his expectant face, and she couldn't refuse. Despite her earlier misgivings, she could now see Steven was a nice man. She picked up a couple of the chocolates in their red and black wrappings and put them in her coat pocket.

"Thanks. I'll have some later."

TWENTY-TWO

Eighteen years ago

It was a rainy, cold night. Raindrops lashed against the windows, and thunder rumbled in the distant sky. Connie had locked herself in the bathroom and turned the tap on so Jeffrey wouldn't hear.

"You wouldn't dare do that," Connie whispered, fear curdling into nausea in the pit of her stomach.

"Oh no? Try me. Tomorrow, when you pick up Chloe from nursery, she won't be there."

"The nursery staff will never release Chloe to you. You're not a guardian, and a stranger needs to know the password." The nurseries had a system for identifying relatives apart from the mother. The password was the most commonly used method.

"You don't think I know the password?" The man let out a short laugh, and the sound chilled Connie's heart. "Jeffrey picked Chloe up from nursery last night, didn't he? I bet he didn't check the man standing behind him. He thought I was just another dad coming to pick up his child."

Connie thought she might faint. She felt dizzy and sat down on the edge of the bathtub.

"I know the password," the man said. "It's Bentley 1999, isn't it?"

Connie gasped in fright. He was right. "What do you want?" she rasped.

"Come and meet me in Blenheim Hills. Take the turning off Woodstock and go into the hills. There's a road on the left that leads to a farmhouse. I'll be waiting for you there. I want you," he breathed into the phone.

Connie shivered. She faced an impossible choice. She didn't want to see him. The voices remained, but they had become less frequent. The medicine was starting to take effect – although it made her drowsy and also increased her appetite. Dr Patel had told her that was a common side effect. But she didn't care much; she only wanted the voices to stop and to feel less anxious. But first, she had to deal with this man. But how? If she went to the police, he would try to harm Chloe or her mother. He meant business. She could tell Jeffrey, but would that help? Jeffrey might go to the police, and that would make things worse.

She had no choice, she realised. To save Chloe, she had to take extreme measures.

"Okay," she said. "I'll see you there. Send me the exact location."

"If you tell your husband, or the police, or anyone else, Chloe disappears tomorrow. Remember that."

"Don't worry," she said. "I want you as well. I'm sorry, I've not been thinking straight these last few weeks."

He was silent, and she knew he was trying to gauge her sincerity.

"Be there at seven tonight. Don't do anything stupid."

Later, Connie made an excuse about getting some supplies from the grocery store. Jeffrey seemed surprised but didn't stop her. Connie took one last, long look at her husband as he watched TV. He was a good, kind man. He had stood by her despite all her troubles. The determination firmed in her mind, becoming an iron chain. She owed him a better life.

She went out, pulling the hood of her raincoat over her head. She walked briskly to the town centre, feeling the object inside her coat, wrapped up in a towel. She flagged down a taxi and gave the driver the location. In half an hour, the man dropped her off at the mouth of a dirt track. From here, she would walk. Lightning flashed in the sky as the heavens opened up again. Connie climbed steadily up the hill, then saw the lights. The dark shape of the triangular building got clearer as she went up the slope. The smell of rotting weeds and animal waste assaulted her nostrils. There was a fence on the right side of the road, and a gust of wind blew in, taking all the smells away. Rain whispered on her face, and the air was suddenly cleaner, smelling of wind and greenery. She was on a hilltop, and the ground was far below. A door in the farmhouse opened, and the man stepped out. As he got closer, Connie shivered but stood her ground.

"Come in," he said.

They went inside. The farmhouse had seen better days. The floor had caved in, exposing the bare earth below. The timber logs in the walls had rotted, and insects crawled up them. The man walked her into the kitchen.

"Take off your coat," he said.

Connie was now glad she had hidden the knife, wrapped in a towel, down her sock. She took off her coat, and the man hung it up. He took her in his arms. He was handsome, and his dark eyes glimmered in the light. He kissed her, and she didn't resist. His kissing grew more passionate, and she could feel the hardness between his legs. He pushed her against the wall, his hands now roaming all over her body. She stopped him, and he looked at her with a frown on his face.

"Come upstairs? Or somewhere more comfortable?"

He smiled and led her up the stairs. Puffs of dust rose as they went up the creaking old staircase. On the landing, she smelt mildew and more rotting wood. He opened the door and thrust her against the wall again and resumed his passionate kissing.

"I need to go to the loo," she said.

He disengaged and showed her the bathroom opposite the bedroom.

Connie went in and removed the knife from her sock. She unwrapped the towel and held the knife in her hand. She heard a creaking sound outside. Then suddenly, the door was flung open, crashing against the wall. The bathroom shook, and Connie almost fell off the toilet. She held up the knife, but the man had already seen it. He grabbed her wrist with one hand, pushing the knife hand back. Then she was on the floor, and he was on top of her. His strong fingers gripped her throat, and he banged her head against the floor.

"You cunning bitch," he whispered. "You came here to kill me?" He slammed her head against the floor again, and pain mushroomed in her skull like a red fireball. Her vision swam, and she couldn't see. The pressure on her neck grew tighter, her legs thrashed, and she bucked her waist, trying to dislodge him. But he was too strong. His breath was hot on her mouth as he leaned closer.

"Now you'll get what you deserved, you filthy wench."

He grinded her wrist on the wood till she thought it would break. She cried out as her fingers went slack. The knife was in his hands now. He raised it up in the air and plunged it down on her neck. Before she died, Connie heard the whisper in her ear.

"One day, I'll come back for your daughter. Chloe will pay for your sins."

TWENTY-THREE

When Nikki and Monty got back to Kidlington South HQ, the Piersons were waiting for her. They had identified the body, and hadn't been able to go back home, for reasons Nikki didn't fully understand. She had imagined they'd want to be as far away from Oxford as possible. But perhaps that wasn't how Jeffrey Pierson's mind was working at the moment. He wanted answers, and Nikki knew from now on he would be haunted forever by this event.

Nikki and Monty went back to the office first, to catch up with Kristy and Nish. Light was fading from the summer sky, a ring of blue velvet on the rims of the horizon slowly closing in. Nikki felt tired from the day's events, but she also knew the day was far from done.

"Where is Tom?" Nikki asked when she saw the detective sergeant wasn't present.

Kristy and Nish glanced at each other before speaking, and Nikki knew something had happened. Nish sighed.

"He's got troubles with his ex-wife again. He went to pick up the children from her place to take them to school, but she didn't let them out. Apparently, his son's not well, but she won't let him see the boy. He rang to say he's going to be delayed."

"Sounds like my ex-wife," Monty sighed as he lowered himself into a chair. He pulled up another one and lifted his feet onto it. "But that was a long time ago." He raised his arms over his head, stretching. "Maybe I should speak to Tom. These things do get easier with time."

"Yes, time is the best healer," Nikki agreed. She'd had a quiet separation from her ex-husband. He couldn't live with the unsociable work hours of a police inspector. Nikki knew if she had been a man, it would have been different. Women just put up with it, but it wasn't like that when the roles are reversed. She didn't have anything against her ex-husband, and luckily, they had remained friends.

Their daughter Rita's welfare was their priority, and she didn't use her daughter against her ex. She felt sorry for Tom. Whatever the reason for his separation, the children should be protected from it at all costs.

"He might do well to speak to you, guv," Nish said. "He's not having an easy time of it."

"Give me his number," Monty said. "I'll have a word with him… If he talks to me, that is."

"I think he will," Nish said. "You worked with him before, right?"

"In one case, when he was a uniformed constable in North Kidlington. That was a while ago."

Monty glanced at Nish and Kristy. With Nikki, he updated them about their meeting with Jemima.

Nikki asked, "Fiona and Mark are both AWOL, any news on them?"

"Facial recognition software on CCTV cameras around town hasn't shown anything new from last night. They found a few men matching his description, but none were Mark," Kristy said. "I've just been upstairs to look at the images. They're different – three individuals."

"We need to find him quickly," Nikki said. "He can't be far. What did his phone triangulation show?"

"A bar in Cowley. It's not far from where he was last seen on CCTV with Chloe. Chloe's phone signal also triangulated to the same spot."

"So they were both at the same bar in the early evening," Monty said. "Then they must have separated, because according to Jemima, Chloe went for dinner with someone else. She met someone..."

"Could that be why she was having an argument with Mark? Chloe had someone else in her life?" Nish asked.

Nikki frowned. "Something doesn't make sense. Earlier, Mark and Chloe seemed perfectly close on camera, holding hands. That wasn't for our benefit. We're missing something here. Only Mark can clarify it."

"Did Mark have a car?" Monty asked.

"Yes, a Ford Focus, still parked on the street in Summertown, where he lived. He's not been back home. We've got a squad car parked nearby, keeping watch."

"As for Fiona, the DVLA doesn't have a car registered in her name." Kristy clicked on her keyboard and pulled up Fiona's student ID. Her dark eyes were framed by brown hair that went past her shoulders. "Her parents are super wealthy. She comes from the Bartlett dynasty, who own a large advertising business, with several branches all over the UK. I'm surprised she doesn't have a car, to be honest."

"Fiona fancied Mark. Jemima mentioned that. Their friendship was falling apart. She was also on the college grounds later that night." Nikki paused, and everyone looked at her. "Did Chloe fall, or did Fiona push her...?"

"Or maybe Fiona didn't intend to push her. But something happened, and Chloe lost her balance. She fell and died."

The question hung in the air, the silence broken only by their breathing.

Nikki went to her desk and picked up the phone. She called the duty surveillance officer and asked for a car to be stationed outside Fiona's house. Then she called Traffic and told them to patrol around Fiona's and Mark's houses tonight.

"Okay, good." Nikki sighed, thinking hard. It was something Jemima said. "Chloe thought an old man was following her in the club... Who was he?" she mused. "And who did she go to see in Iffley – in that market stall?"

"We looked at the list from the Farmer's Market Association," Nish began. "Not every stall has a name with it. And on the coloured CCTV, we can't see the logo of the stall holder. But businesses that rent stalls have to put their names down. We're going through them, to see if we can find anyone who knows who kept that stall with the blue and white awning."

"That will take some time," Nikki said. She shook her head. Sometimes police work was like that: painstakingly chasing down people and clues when you wanted answers fast. "Treat it as a priority tomorrow. Did you find anything else on the CCTV from the nightclub? An old man with a beard can't be that hard to spot."

Kristy said, "We haven't found anything yet, but we'll keep looking."

Nikki got to her feet and motioned for Monty to follow her. "I'm going to speak with the family and see what they want." She looked at her watch. It was past eight p.m., and it had been a long, exhausting day.

"You two should make your way home."

Nish and Kristy raised their eyebrows at her. They all had a lot more work to do. Nikki walked down the corridor with Monty, heading for the family interview room, where the Piersons were waiting for her.

TWENTY-FOUR

The pale, haggard face of Jeffrey Pierson greeted them when they walked in. The room was meant to be a calm sanctuary for troubled families, but Nikki didn't see any peace in Jeffrey's eyes. The storm was raging inside him. His fingers twitched as he clutched his knees, leaning forward.

"Any news, Inspector?"

"We're finding out more about Chloe with every passing minute." In brief, Nikki told them what she had learned from Sally and Jemima. "I'm afraid Chloe was under the influence of drugs last night. As to what exactly, the pathologist will know in a couple of days when the toxicology results are back. In that case, an accident is more than likely."

Jeffrey blinked a few times. His face remained stuck in the rigid grasp of grief. "So you're ruling out foul play? She wasn't pushed?"

"At this stage, we have to keep our minds open. We don't know for sure how many people were in the college grounds late last night. The CCTV shows the college students coming back around one in the morning. Chloe came back just before them. She was on her own. In the group of students, I'm not sure if there were any strangers. We need to analyse the footage more. If we find anything, we'll let you know."

Monty asked, "Did Chloe ever mention knowing an older man? Someone with a white beard?"

Jeffrey looked puzzled, and glanced at Angela, who shrugged. "I'm afraid I don't know what you're talking about. Who's this old man?"

"We don't know. But we have reason to think Chloe knew him."

Nikki spoke up. "Did Chloe known anyone in a village called Iffley? It's close to Oxford. Did she have any friends there?"

The couple frowned as they thought. Then Jeffrey shook his head again. "Not that Chloe told me. Why? Did she go there?"

"A couple of times, yes. We saw her on CCTV. She went to the high street and market. Iffley doesn't have a lot of CCTV, so she could've gone elsewhere as well. We don't know. But we're looking into it."

Jeffrey's face remained blank. Angela reached out a hand and gripped his. He clung on at her touch.

Nikki's mind went back to the photo of Chloe's mother. Chloe had been too young to remember her mother, and it was a loss she carried in her heart. Hence the photo on the shelf. Nikki didn't know why, but she felt there was a significance here, an angle she couldn't quite grasp. The vague outline of a shape she couldn't recognise. It bothered her.

"Did Chloe ask you about her mother? Recently, I mean."

Jeffrey was surprised by the question. He licked his dry lower lip.

"As a matter of fact, she did. A couple of months ago, I think it was. She wanted to know where exactly Connie was last seen. It was in the hills near Blenheim, west of Oxford. I went there a few times, with the police, when Connie disappeared. Many years ago, when Chloe was a teenager, she wanted to see the place."

"How did the police know she was there?" Nikki asked. Her mind was moving, flowing like a river in high tide. "Witnesses?"

"No. It was dark when she left. She took a cab and the police found her on CCTV. They got hold of the cab driver, and he told them where he dropped her off. The police suspected the cab driver for a long time. But it wasn't him."

"You lived in Wolvercote at the time, correct?"

"Yes."

Nikki looked at Monty, and she knew he was on the same page. Wolvercote was in North Oxford, and the case would've been dealt with by Thames Valley Police.

"And the police assumed she was dead? But her body was never found?" Nikki asked, a sharpness in her words.

"Yes, and yes. It's mostly farmland up there, with the gentle hills you normally see in the Cotswolds. But some hills have sharp drops. They assumed she fell."

Nikki lapsed into silence. Monty asked, "How was your wife before she disappeared? Mentally, I mean."

"She wasn't great, but she'd started on medication, and she was starting to get stable again. She was a troubled person, as you know. But she doted on Chloe. She'd never leave her daughter."

"What was she like in the weeks before the event?" Monty persisted.

Nikki looked at him, trying to gauge where was going with this. Jeffrey shrugged. "She could be anxious and sad, a lot of the time. But we had happy times as well." He paused, frowning. "Those days, she used to sleep in the daytime. Not always, but sometimes I used to come back from work and see her passed out on the sofa. Chloe would be at nursery."

"How long did the police investigation continue for?"

"A year, almost." Jeffrey shook his head, and Angela

clutched his hand. "It never left me. To this day, I think of what happened that night. What demons had possessed her."

"I know you've been through this already," Nikki said. "But can you think of anyone that Constance used to see or visit in those days? Or did you suspect her of having an affair?"

"She was the quiet type. She had some friends, but she didn't see them that frequently. The police talked to all of them. Nothing was found. As for an affair?" Jeffrey spread his palms and raised his eyebrows. "I don't know. She had the opportunity, I guess, as I worked most of the time. I had to travel with work as well and stay in Leeds. That happened for a few weeks before she disappeared."

"So she was by herself then," Nikki echoed. "We will look into Constance's case again. I don't think there's a link," she said to reassure Jeffrey. But she wasn't so sure herself. A little mouse of discomfort kept gnawing at the back of her skull. "But we would like to know more about Connie."

Nikki asked, "What did Chloe ask you a couple of months ago?"

"She wanted to visit the spot again," he said. "She went there with Mark. They paid their respects, I think. I'm not sure; you'll have to ask Mark."

Nikki nodded and glanced at Monty. His forehead was creased, and he was listening intently.

Jeffrey looked animated suddenly. "I just remembered something. Chloe found one of her mother's diaries in the loft. She asked me if Connie knew a man called Steven. I wasn't aware of anyone with that name."

Nikki leaned forward. "Steven? Did she give you a last name?"

"No."

"And what about the diary?" Nikki glanced at Monty. In their thorough search of Chloe's room, they hadn't found a diary that sounded similar.

"She kept it. I didn't see it." Jeffrey glanced at Angela, who also shook her head in denial.

Nikki felt the diary was important. "So Chloe took the diary back with her to Oxford?"

"Yes," Angela said. "We didn't see it in the house. We looked through the stuff in her room."

Nikki looked at Jeff. "Did you know what Connie might have written in the diary? Did she ever share it with you?"

"I'm sorry, no."

A shape was gathering form in Nikki's mind, but it still remained out of focus, hazy. "Can you please have a look once again? In the attic, or anywhere you might not have looked. If you can find the diary, or anything similar from Connie, please send it to us."

Jeff nodded, a new understanding in his eyes. "Yes, of course."

TWENTY-FIVE

Eight weeks ago

Steven Pugh paced his room in the darkness. He dared not put the light on. He stopped at the window and peered out. The streetlights were coming on and he could see a neighbour walking down to his house. He watched the street for strangers all the time now.

After Chloe had visited his stall in the market, alarm bells had started ringing like a claxon.

That bitch. How did she find him?

She was resourceful and clever – and therefore, dangerous. Luckily, his charm offensive had worked. She believed him – or at least he thought so.

She had taken a couple of the special chocolates. That made him smile. Maybe she wasn't so clever after all... Deep inside, she might be as vulnerable as her mother was. Connie... That was a blast from the past. But Steven never forgot his victims.

He liked to go for the needy, weak ones, the ones who came from stable middle-class homes. They were more of a challenge.

Clarissa had been a challenge. She'd been a little high and

mighty at first. But he didn't lose any time working his charms, getting her hooked on his drug. Once she was a heroin addict, there was no going back. He got her pregnant, kept her hooked on the stuff, made her give up her son. Yes, his son. Well, he never wanted a child, did he? Why did that silly bitch not use protection? Not his fault. As far as he was concerned, it was good that the boy went to the care home. He couldn't look after the child, and Clarissa... well, Clarissa was hooked on heroin so badly then she could barely look after herself.

But then she got rid of him, before he could get rid of her, for good. She met that other man, who looked after her. Well, no regrets. Through Clarissa he met an even juicier target.

Constance. Connie. His wispy, dreamy, doe-eyed Connie. Tender to a fault, broken like a chainsaw had run through every bone in her body. Her mental health meant she was always fragile. It didn't take him long to realise he could do what he wanted with Connie. All he had to do was make her an addict.

Shooting up into the veins... there was no purer pleasure. Especially when he injected himself with water, while giving her the real stuff. He watched with fascination as Connie's paranoid psychosis went from bad to worse. Her only relief was in heroin, in the hit that turned her world to dark night. And she came to him for that. He was controlling her, changing the narrative of her life, just as he liked it.

But Connie also changed. She understood, and wanted to move on. That's when he knew he couldn't let her go. Not like Clarissa.

He had enjoyed dragging Connie out that night. She had come to his lair, and he still thought a part of her had wanted to do it. Just like Clarissa. And his other victims. All women, all vulnerable, all with a dark core in their hearts that he exposed. All of us have it, don't we? That dark, silent beast in our souls. It lies dormant, but Steven knew how to unleash it. Once its fangs were bared, it wanted more blood. There was no going back. That excited him beyond all measure.

But then... then they wanted to move on like he didn't matter. No, he couldn't let that happen. Clarissa got lucky, Connie wouldn't.

Steven went to his mother's bedroom. He had kept her room like a mausoleum. Everything was in its place – the Zimmer frame by the bed, pill bottle on the bedside table. Every morning he filled up the jug of water and placed it on the table. He put a light on and fluffed up the pillows like she would appear out of nowhere and start to read her book. Those crime thrillers she enjoyed so much. Yes, he thought his mother came back to this room.

He always kept the blinds drawn and the window shut. It was stuffy inside, but he didn't care. Her photos adorned the sideboard, and the desk. He'd wanted to keep her dead body, but he knew embalming was illegal in the UK. Oh well. He could still keep the room as a shrine.

He thought of the times his mother had beat him with a stick, chucked him down the basement stairs. But she also loved him, he knew she did. He needed to be tough, she said, that's why she beat him as a child.

He now went to her bedside and sank down with hands folded, like he was praying.

"Mama, this girl came to the stall today. Her name's Chloe, and she says she's Connie's daughter. I need to get rid of her, don't I?"

He imagined his mother sickly, pasty face as she lay there, dying. Just like Connie's face had looked. His mother opened her mouth, her dead eyes staring upward, unfocused.

Get rid of her, she whispered.

"Yes, Mother. I will."

TWENTY-SIX

Nikki flopped down on her chair in the office and sighed. It was half eight at night, and her stomach was rumbling. She stifled a yawn.

Her eyes were tired from reading the case report into Constance Pierson's disappearance. Jeffrey was right, the cab driver had been the main suspect. But he hadn't had Connie's DNA on him. CCTV didn't show him near Connie's house, and Connie had never been in his car before. He didn't have a history of taking women in his car, and his movements were checked with the cab company. In short, after a few months he was no longer a suspect.

And his name wasn't Steven. Nikki had written that name in her diary and circled it.

Connie's medical notes were interesting. She'd had a condition called psychotic depression and often heard voices, so was on medication from a psychiatrist. Nikki leaned forward, rubbing her exhausted, painful eyes as she read the GP notes.

Two weeks before her vanishing, Connie had seen her GP, Dr Jaya Patel. She had confessed to being addicted to temazepam, a drug often used for anxiety and as a sleeping pill. Nikki knew these drugs often ended up in the street market, sold as narcotics. It was easy to get addicted to them.

Connie said she was getting them from a friend, but no names were mentioned. That meeting with Dr Patel was the last time that Connie saw her doctor. Dr Patel had examined her and noted that Connie appeared to have a cold. Her pulse rate and blood pressure were high, but she didn't have a fever.

Nikki looked through Connie's medical records but couldn't find another instance of her approaching Dr Patel about her temazepam addiction. These addictions took time to develop – months, in fact. How long had Connie been on the drugs? And what if she took other drugs as well?

Like mother, like daughter? Nikki thought grimly. Chloe took drugs too, and that was probably the reason for her death.

The door opened, and Monty came in.

"You should go home," Monty said. He stood with his feet spread apart and thrust his hands inside his pockets. "I'll go and check if Traffic have found anything on CCTV about Mark. Do you want to put out an all-points bulletin for him?" An APB would mean Mark's passport and driving licence would be flagged at every harbour and airport in the UK, and his details shared with every police force in the country.

Nikki pressed both hands to her temples, massaging them. A headache was threatening, and the pressure from her fingers felt good.

"I'm not sure if that's necessary at this stage. Mark's a suspect, certainly, but if I put out an APB, I have to justify it. Chances are, we can find him tomorrow. His car's still there. Have we checked his bank cards?"

Monty looked at the empty desks of the two detective constables.

"Kristy and Nish should have followed up on that by now. I guess we'll find out tomorrow."

Monty stretched his long arms over his head, his fingertips almost brushing the ceiling. He flexed his shoulders, and the joints cracked.

"Let me go and check with Traffic upstairs. Do you want to wait?"

Nikki thought he'd left something unsaid and looked at him. "Yes," she replied. "I've got to prepare a report for Patmore anyway. Do you want a coffee?"

The door opened, and the detective constables entered. Both of them looked tired.

"Still here?" Nikki asked. "Thought you'd be home by now."

Kristy's cheeks were rosy, and her eyes were shining.

"Wait till you see this, guv. We just got CCTV back from New College." Kristy sat down at her desk and pulled up a laptop. The others crowded around, and Kristy played the footage on her screen. The date was the third of June, yesterday.

Kristy's attention was on the screen. "What time did you say the girls returned from the nightclub?"

"Forty three minutes past midnight. I've got them here. The light isn't great, but I think that's Jemima I can see."

The others gathered around her desk again as Kristy highlighted the faces. "They're passing under some lights," Kristy said. She zoomed in and circled the faces of the four women. Nikki recognised the third one.

"That's Fiona, isn't it?"

"Yes. And the others are Jemima and Chloe. There are two other girls I don't recognise," Monty added.

"They must be the ones Jemima mentioned who went back upstairs with her. Can we see what time this group left the grounds?"

Kristy located the camera over the halls of residence. "At one am." She paused the footage. A group of girls were seen entering, and then the door shut behind them. "I can see only three," Kristy said, "and neither Fiona nor Chloe are there."

Nikki straightened, troubled voices whispering in her mind. "That settles it. Fiona was definitely out there with Chloe last night.

TWENTY-SEVEN

Monty offered to give Nikki a lift back to her place in Kidlington – and she was more than happy to be a passenger this evening after an exhausting day.

The familiar turmoil returned as she walked to his car, feeling his presence alongside her. Would she, or wouldn't she?

When she looked at Monty, saw his sharp chestnut eyes resting on her, she felt the urgent longing. She couldn't remember the last time she had been with a man. It had been before she came to Oxford. Since then, a combination of work and family had kept her mind occupied, and her bed remained empty. She couldn't lie to herself – it would be nice to have a strong, warm man next to her.

They reached the car, and she strapped herself into the passenger seat. Monty started the car but didn't reverse immediately. In the half-light, she stared back at him.

"Straight home, or shall we stop for a drink?" he asked and his cheeks dimpled in a smile.

It was just a drink, she thought. What harm would a drink do?

"All right then," she said. "But you're only having one, Monty. You're driving back home."

Bright lights festooned the trees around the country pub, giving it a festive atmosphere and people were making the most of the balmy evening sat outside on benches.

The aroma of roasted meat and potatoes hit as they went inside and Nikki realised just how hungry she was. Her fridge was empty – it would be just cheese and crackers until tomorrow, unless—

"The food here is excellent – it's a gastropub." He'd read her mind.

Nikki studied him. "Bring all your dates here, do you?"

"Only the special ones."

Nikki raised her eyebrows and Monty's face softened. He leaned closer, his face animated, the scent of his aftershave still present after a long day's work.

"Hey, I was just joking."

"I don't mind," she said. She held his eyes in a frank gaze. "Your life is your business, right?"

He gazed at her like he was trying to discern the meaning behind her words. Then he nodded. "I guess so."

He turned away as the bartender approached, and Nikki realised she had ignored the menu. She chose her dish, and they ordered.

"So, how's Emily?" Nikki asked, referring to Monty's sixteen-year-old daughter.

Monty took a long sip of his beer. "She's good. But I'm still a bit worried about the company she keeps. I smell the smoke on her when she comes back."

"We did the same things when we were teenagers. Where does she go out to?"

"Nightclubs in Oxford, and also in the towns around. A nightspot becomes well-known, and all the young people go there. I've picked her up a couple of times when she's called me at two in the morning. Daddy's cab service." Monty rolled his eyes, then smiled.

"Surprised you don't go inside and check up on her," Nikki said. "She might discover you one day. That would go down well."

Monty grimaced, and Nikki laughed. Then she got serious. "Has she been to Cargo? The club Chloe went to?"

"I asked her, and she said no. Her friends have been though, and she has plans to visit. I've told her to stay away. Didn't tell her why, obviously."

"Has she taken drugs?"

Monty sighed. "I don't know. I've had a frank discussion with her. If she's taking drugs, I've told her she can talk to me. She confessed she's smoked some cannabis. Apart from that, I suspect she's taken other substances as well, but I can't be sure."

"If you're picking her up from the nightclubs, I doubt that. She'd be wanting to stay out the whole night and get back home much later, maybe even at seven in the morning. That's when the after-parties break up on the weekend."

"Voice of experience, are you? You did say you used to go clubbing in your younger days."

"Yes, a long time ago. I guess there's a time and place for everything – I don't mind letting my hair down once in a while. Why not?"

"Why not indeed," Monty echoed in his clipped, Oxonian English. Sometimes, he sounded posher than an aristocrat. "I can see you out clubbing, actually. Dancing the night away." He grinned over the rim of his glass, and his eyes twinkled.

"Maybe we should have a team night out. Kristy and Nish would know where to go."

"That's an excellent idea. We should plan for it. How's Rita doing, by the way?"

Nikki hadn't seen Rita for a week, and she was missing her. It wasn't her weekend, and Rita had to wait almost another week before she saw her teenager again.

Rita was now in the first year of her A levels, and Nikki knew that in a couple of years' time, university life would sweep her away, and she would see less and less of her daughter. She didn't want to let go, and she knew she felt insecure because she only saw Rita every other weekend. Following the divorce and the move to Oxford, she had no other choice. Rita's life was in London, and she was thriving. That was the only thing that mattered.

"She's good. Working hard for her end-of-year assessments. She's stressing, but her teachers think she will be fine."

"Will she apply to Oxford?"

"Yes." Nikki's heart did a dance of pride and happiness. "She wants to study English Lit. Let's see what happens, eh?"

"I hope that works out," Monty said. "Your mum's also here and she'd love it if Rita got into Oxford, wouldn't she?"

"Yes." That reminded Nikki. She took out her phone and clicked her tongue when she saw the missed calls from Clarissa. Her mother had sent her a text in the morning to say she wanted to speak. Nikki had forgotten all about it, and now Clarissa had tried to call.

"You mind if I quickly call my mother? I'm sorry."

Monty spread his hands. "We've gone past all that formality, haven't we?" He waved a hand. "Go and call her now."

Nikki went to the door and stepped outside. She stood against the wall, a safe distance from the other punters. Clarissa answered on the first ring.

"Nikki, is that you?"

"Yes, Mum, it's me. Sorry it took so long to call you back. Is anything the matter?"

Clarissa was silent for a while, and Nikki didn't like it. "I got an envelope through the letterbox today. It didn't have any postage stamps or address. It was addressed to me." Clarissa was silent again.

"Well, what was it?" Nikki asked.

"A box of chocolates, but it was empty. Like the ones you get in the supermarket, nothing special."

"An empty box of chocolates? And it was in an envelope?"

"Yes. It's the most peculiar thing. I don't know why anyone would bother. Maybe one of the street kids is playing a prank. They know I live alone."

Nikki's mind raced. Her mother lived in Jericho, a nice neighbourhood in North Oxford. She didn't think the children on the street would be doing this – but it was a possibility.

Clarissa had lived in a derelict house and smoked and drunk herself into poor health. It was only a few months ago that Nikki had reconnected with her mother. The truth about Tommy's disappearance had resolved some of Clarissa's fractured past and reunited Nikki with her. She was glad their relationship was good, and they had left the past behind.

"It's probably nothing. Someone made a mistake. Make sure you lock all the doors and windows at night. I'll come round tomorrow morning before work, and we can examine the envelope."

"Okay," Clarissa said. "I'll see you tomorrow."

Nikki went back to the table and saw their food had arrived. Monty was standing, rubbing his lower back. He looked at her questioningly.

"Everything okay?"

They sat down. "Yes, she's all right," Nikki said. "She got a funny envelope in the post." Nikki told Monty about the empty chocolate box as they ate.

"How weird... How old was the box? And was it expensive?"

"I don't know. I'll find these things out when I see her tomorrow. I could've taken fingerprints, but she's opened it now. Maybe it's just a prank."

"I'm sure it is." Monty shovelled a slice of chicken into his mouth.

Nikki nodded, still distracted by the strange news.

Monty had been right. The food was gorgeous. Nikki had baked cod with chorizo, and the fish was done to perfection. The side dish of vegetables was also excellent. She finished with a sigh of satisfaction and watched Monty pat his belly.

"Happy?" he asked.

She nodded, and his eyes twinkled, then his lips relaxed.

"You're the first person I've brought here, by the way. No one else." He waved a hand. "Emily and I have been once for Sunday lunch. But that's it."

They stared at each other, unflinching. She understood the significance of his words. There was no one else in his life. He had mentioned it in passing before, but now she knew for sure.

They shared the bill and left. Monty stood by the door as she opened it. She turned around.

"Good night," she said.

TWENTY-EIGHT

Nikki was exhausted. She closed the door after saying goodbye to Monty, and her house welcomed her with its familiar silence, broken only by the gentle hum of the refrigerator. She'd left a lamp on a timer switch in the living room – a habit she'd developed over more than twenty years on the force. Empty houses shouldn't look empty, especially at night. She also checked the windows in the kitchen and ground floor to make sure nothing had been tampered with – another old habit.

Nikki's hands trembled slightly as she filled the kettle – too much coffee, too little sleep. Steam from the shower would help. It always did.

In the bathroom upstairs, she peeled off her work clothes, leaving them in an untidy heap on the floor. The hot water pounded against her shoulders, and she closed her eyes, trying to wash away the memory of Chloe's face. But it clung to her like the steam on the mirror, refusing to evaporate.

Fifteen minutes later, wrapped in her thick dressing gown, Nikki padded back into the kitchen. The evening air had grown cooler, and something felt different about the house. Her eyes swept across the dining room, her instincts cutting through the fatigue. The window was open, curtains stirring in the breeze.

She froze, water from her hair dripping onto the dressing gown. That window had been closed. She was certain. Or was she? Fatigue had played tricks on her before, made her doubt simple things.

Nikki phone lay on the kitchen counter, screen dark.

A sound broke through the silence – a soft scraping, like metal against wood. It came from outside, near the back of the house. Her pulse quickened. She killed the kitchen lights and moved to the side window, keeping to the shadows. She saw a shape hunched outside the window, hands working at the window sill. She stifled a scream, but the man heard her. He looked up. A balaclava covered his face. Only the eyes and nose were visible. He watched her intently, then slowly stepped back. Fear had rooted Nikki's feet to the floor.

The man kept his eyes on her. As if he was trying to communicate with her in silence. Nikki wished she had her extendable baton on her – and her clothes on. Her hands became claws. What would she do if the man attacked her?

Slowly, he took a step back. He watched her still, enjoying her predicament. The streetlight caught the side of his face, throwing half of it into sharp relief. He wasn't trying to hide.

Nikki reached for her phone with trembling fingers, never taking her eyes off the man.

He tilted his head, studying her house. Studying her. She could feel his gaze even through the darkness, as if the walls between them had become transparent. Her fingers were frozen on the phone's screen like the rest of her body.

Then he moved backwards, melting into the shadows between the houses. Nikki counted her heartbeats – one, two, three, four – before racing to shut the window. The man was running – but he was slow. His gait was slightly lopsided to the left. A memory struck her. Where had she seen someone move like that? And then he was gone.

She stood in the silence of her house, listening to the sound of her own breathing. Her wet hair had soaked through her dressing gown, making her shiver.

The wind rustled through the now-closed dining room window, and Nikki felt the weight of the empty house around her.

She lifted the phone to her ear and told the 999 operator she had an intruder in the house. When she was connected to the police, the duty officer recognised her name and that she was from the major investigation team.

"Are you DI Gill of the MIT in South Kid?"

"Yes," Nikki answered in a hollow, unfeeling voice. Adrenaline was still surging through her body like electricity, but she felt burnt out, empty. The officer took her details and promised to send a car ASAP.

She went to her room and got dressed. She got her baton, and gripping it tightly, went around the rest of the house, flicking all the lights on. Then she sat down on the sofa, her breathing still fast and jerky. She called Monty.

"I'm on my way. Stay there, lock everything, and don't move."

Monty arrived just after the police did. She wouldn't admit it, but it was good to see him. She joined Monty and the two uniformed officers as they searched the garden, and the neighbour's house.

"I'm staying here," Monty said, after they got back inside. He raised a hand when she tried to speak. "Or you come with me and stay at mine." From the hard set of his jaw, she knew he wouldn't take no for an answer.

"Fine." She sighed, again, secretly glad someone was staying with her. "You can sleep on the couch, or there's the other bedroom upstairs."

"The couch is fine, if you have some bedding."

She opened a bottle of wine after making Monty's makeshift bed and offered him a glass. He refused.

"Don't want booze to dull my senses. You get to sleep."

There was a steely look in his eyes. Monty was going to keep guard tonight, and he was angry at what had happened. She was too numb with a cocktail of emotions to know exactly what she felt. She drained her glass. Then she went upstairs and crashed into bed. Sleep didn't come easily, and when it did, strange dreams tormented her.

TWENTY-NINE

Nikki was woken by knocking on the door. Someone was calling her name. It was Monty. She woke up with a start. Daylight streamed in through the crack in the curtains. She flung the covers off and stumbled to the door. Monty's knocking was giving her a headache.

He stood back when she opened the door. He looked tired, stubbled cheeks sunken.

Monty sighed. "You okay?"

She stifled a yawn. "As well as I can be." Last night's events hung over her like a cloud. "Thanks for staying last night."

"No problem. I slept alright actually. Nice couch." He grinned.

Nikki got ready while Monty used the loo downstairs. She made him breakfast, and they agreed to meet at the station.

"Thank you," Nikki said, at the door. "You didn't have to do that. I would've been okay."

"I know. I knew that guy wouldn't come back. But I also know what it's like to be alone after a shock."

"You do?"

He exhaled. "Maybe a discussion for another day. But my ex-wife got me arrested on a fake charge of domestic violence."

"What?"

"Yup. I was handcuffed in front of my daughter and taken to the station. No one could believe it was me. My ex had no evidence of course, and there was no previous accusation. She also didn't push for a conviction – she just wanted to get me arrested to teach me a lesson. Can you believe it?"

"Oh Monty. I'm sorry."

He sighed and squared his shoulders. "It was hard. I was home in a few hours, but I was shaken that night. Couldn't sleep a wink. I lived alone then. One of my mates came to stay and chat. Not the same situation as you, of course. Yours was worse. That's why I... Never mind, I better go."

Nikki watched Monty as he slowly trudged to his car. Everyone had their demons. No one was an exception. Monty got in the car and waved, and she waved back.

She went upstairs and got ready. Suddenly, her mind went to Clarissa, and her strange package. She'd promised to go over to see her mum before she went to work, and now it felt more urgent than ever.

It was seven in the morning, and Clarissa wasn't answering her phone. Nikki had pressed the doorbell twice and waited. No response. She looked around the small front garden. Her mother lived in a semi-detached cottage dating back to the eighteenth century. It had fallen into disrepair, with damp in the walls, but in the last few months, with Nikki's help, Clarissa had made an effort. The front lawn was now well-trimmed, and Clarissa had planted a flowerbed along the borders. Rita had chosen the flowers. It had been a fun time, all three of them working together to patch up Clarissa's house.

Nikki knocked on the door again, then opened the flap of

the letterbox and called her mother's name. She needed to get to work and Clarissa knew she was coming. However, her mother had never been an early riser and age had only made matters worse. Clarissa could sometimes stay in bed until almost midday. She was getting a little worried and was considering jumping over the side gate when she heard shuffling steps inside. A moment later, the door opened.

Clarissa was clearly just out of bed. Her eyelids were heavy, and her hair straggly. She wore a gown and cardigan and shivered as if she were cold.

"I thought you were coming later," she said.

Nikki walked past her and into the front living room. "You knew when I was coming. I have to go to work."

She looked at her mother. Clarissa yawned and then ambled towards the kitchen. "Can I get you a cuppa?"

Clarissa looked okay, unphased, Nikki thought. The house was neat and clean, photos stacked on shelves, papers and magazines folded under the coffee table. There weren't bottles of gin or overflowing ashtrays anymore. The place looked new after they had ripped up the carpets and painted the walls. She was glad that Clarissa was looking after it.

"Where is it?" Nikki called out, her eyes scanning the room. "That envelope you told me about."

Clarissa appeared at the kitchen doorway. "Oh, it's here, by the side." She went to the mirror on the wall and pulled out a small wooden box from beneath the table.

Nikki stopped her from opening the box and snapped on sterile gloves. Then Clarissa lifted the lid. She pointed to the white envelope, which had only Clarissa's first name written on it. Nikki picked up the envelope and felt the rectangular package inside. It was light. She turned the envelope around.

Apart from Clarissa's name, there was nothing else. She pulled out the chocolate box. It was old. The corners were frayed and ripped and the golden colour had faded to yellow.

The green lettering was chipped in most places. Slowly, Nikki rested the box on the coffee table.

She focused on the envelope, lifting it to the sunlight, but couldn't see any watermarks. She took out a lighter and held the flame near the paper, just close enough for the heat to reveal any invisible ink. Nothing.

Her mother's name was written in block capital letters on the envelope. As Clarissa had said, there were no addresses, or postage stamps.

"Were you at home when this arrived?"

"No," Clarissa shouted back from the kitchen. "I was out doing my shopping. I came back and thought it was a delivery, you know? Instead, I found that weird thing inside."

Clarissa came back into the front room with two steaming cups of tea. She placed them on the coffee table, next to the envelope and empty box.

Nikki said, "Mum, I want you to think carefully. Have you seen anyone new on the street? Someone who might have been looking at your house, or caught your attention?"

Clarissa sipped her tea and narrowed her eyes. "No. There haven't been any new people moving in, and it's the same old crowd as always. Lots of families too. Nothing's changed."

"What about any new cars parked outside? Or vans?"

Clarissa shook her head, then shrugged. "I don't go out that much. I go shopping, and once a week I go to the day centre to meet my friends."

Nikki nodded slowly. She hadn't seen her mother for more than a week, and that was a mistake. She should have stopped by. But on weekdays, Nikki only had time in the evenings, and Clarissa didn't like to be disturbed late.

She pointed at the box of chocolates. "Does that mean anything to you? It looks like it's been lying around for years."

"Exactly. Someone's taken it out of a bin, I think. I mean, who would keep an empty box of chocolates like that?"

"And you're sure it was posted through the letterbox while you were out?"

"Yes, of course, I'm sure," Clarissa sounded indignant. The lines on her forehead grew deeper, knotting together. "Why are you asking?"

"It's just such a strange thing to happen."

Nikki stared at her mother. She always wondered if the years of heavy drinking had softened Clarissa's brain or brought on early dementia. So far, she hadn't seen any signs. Clarissa used to act like she couldn't look after herself, but the real problem had been her guilt and depression over Tommy. She was very different now, but Nikki couldn't help the same thoughts recurring. Still, perhaps Nikki was wrong. Her eyes fell back on the empty box. The plastic surface was ripped in several places, and little gold rings which had held the small chocolate pieces in place were visible. She could see the smudged brown marks on the white paper.

"Okay, keep an eye out for anyone watching the house or acting suspiciously. If you do, can you take a photo?"

"I'll watch from the upstairs windows as well."

"Just let me know, okay?"

Clarissa nodded. Nikki chatted with her mother for a few more minutes, then called a cab to take her to Kidlington. As she waited for the cab outside, Nikki walked up and down the street, her eyes on the few pedestrians who walked past, and the windows of the houses. The oddness of the event lay like a layer of oil on the troubled waters of her mind. Why would anyone send a package like that to Clarissa? Was it a message? About what?

When the cab came, and Nikki sat in the back as the car drove away, her mind remained on the strange paradox, and she worried that Clarissa was omitting something, or choosing not to tell her.

THIRTY

It was eight a.m. when Nikki strode into the open-plan office and the "shop floor" was already busy with activity. Detectives were chatting at each other's desks, and others were engrossed in their screens. Two officers walked past Nikki, and she said hello.

Nikki walked down the side corridor to her office and, as she took her warrant card and radio out from her handbag, Monty followed her in.

"You alright?"

"Yes." She felt closer to him, and wanted to give him a hug, but it would be unprofessional. "Thanks for last night."

Monty waved it off. Then he grinned and pointed a finger at her. "If I'm in a spot of bother I might just call on you."

"I'll be there in a shot," she said, meaning every word. Loyalty mattered to Nikki more than anything else.

"Did you recognise the man, by any chance?" Monty got straight back to work matters, and Nikki was glad. She was still shaken from last night, and her gut told her it was to do with Chloe's death. She didn't know why but she felt it deep in her bones.

"No," Nikki frowned. "But something about his gait was familiar. He had a slight limp on the left. For the life of me, I can't remember where I last saw it."

"Hopefully CCTV will pick him up somewhere. If this man is connected to Chloe, he made a mistake by coming to your house. What did he want?"

Nikki stared at him. "Could he be the one who left the note in Chloe's pocket? '*Ask DI Nikki Gill what happened*'?"

Monty held her gaze, then nodded slowly. "How are you connected to the case? And to Chloe?"

Nikki looked at the brown carpeted floor. She wished the patterns held an answer for her. "I wish I knew. I don't know anything about Chloe. Or her parents. It's just bizarre."

"And this guy didn't seem like just some burglar, did he? He wanted to see you, or scare you?"

"Yes." Nikki looked back at him. "It's like he was trying to tell me something, even if it meant he'd get caught." She shivered. She wouldn't forget that dark figure, watching her from outside the window.

The door opened and Kristy and Nish came in holding steaming mugs of coffee. They sat down at the desk and organised themselves.

"No sign of Mark Ofori yet," Nish began. "We might have to spread his image to the neighbouring towns. I have a feeling he's escaped already."

"Someone is helping him..."

Monty hooked both thumbs on his waistband. The man was built like a cliff – hard and flat. Nikki knew he went to the gym regularly and looked after himself. "We can put the Botley Road gang under surveillance. Paul Diggins, one of their leaders, still lives in Botley near the canal. It's not far from Cowley – Chloe and Mark could have gone to his house the night of her death."

"Yes." Nikki tapped her fingers on the sides of her armchair.

"He'd have to be someone important for them to help him like that, but it's worth looking into."

Monty pulled up a chair and sat down. "I'm not sure... Mark's been in trouble before, but he doesn't have a police record. But sometimes organised crime networks find that attractive. He's a clean skin, so to speak. He'd fly under law enforcement's radar if he distributed their drugs for them – could get large amounts from the gang and use a selection of students as his supply network."

"Like Chloe and Fiona?"

"Exactly. There might be others – we don't know."

"Fiona could be with Mark."

She tapped the pen on a blank page of her black leather notebook. "I'm concerned about the other girls... Jemima and Sally. Jemima mentioned a girl called Kelly who went out with them. Let's put them under surveillance. Can we ask the porters' lodge to keep an eye on their movements: when they go in and out of the college, who they hang around with. If they're meeting up with dodgy people like the Botley Road Boys, I want to know."

Kristy opened her up her laptop. "I spoke to the security manager at the nightclub, he said they hadn't seen an older man with a white beard so far. Nish and I've looked through the footage from Cargo. We couldn't find an old man with a beard, guv, sorry."

"Well done for trying." Nikki smiled at them, aware the duo had arrived here early to scan the rest of the CCTV footage.

Nikki paused and caught Monty's eyes. She exhaled, preparing herself, "There's something else you need to know..." She filled them in on her ordeal.

"Guv, that's awful," Nish exclaimed. "We need to guard your house."

"DI Sen was there last night," Nikki said. "He came with the patrol."

"You should've called us as well," Nish said.

Nikki smiled. It was sweet of them. They hadn't worked together for long but already they were a closely knit team.

"Thank you, but I'll be okay. But yes, I do need a patrol outside my house. At least until we finish this case."

"You think your house intruder is related to the case?" Nish and Kristy were looking at her expectantly.

"Well, I've been personally involved in this case from the beginning. We found a note inside Chloe's coat pocket. It mentioned my name." Nikki told them about the note. "DSU Patmore knows, as does DI Sen. And now you two. I want you to keep this confidential. Got it?" Nikki felt she could trust these two.

The constables nodded. "No one will know from us, guv," Kristy reassured her.

Nikki's phone rang, and she answered. It was Dr Raman, the pathologist.

"I've got the reports back on toxicology," Dr Raman said. "I was going to come and see you, but I don't think this can wait."

THIRTY-ONE

Nikki heard the urgency in Dr Raman's voice. "Go on," she said, and put her on the loudspeaker. "The team is here as well," Nikki explained to the pathologist.

Dr Raman said, "I know the toxicologist at John Radcliffe Hospital. He called me early this morning. Chloe had cocaine in her nostril, and a low amount in her blood stream. Cocaine traces were also found in her hair follicles. But that wasn't the main concern, as the levels were low. We found much higher concentrations of an entirely new chemical, one that my friend has never seen before. And he's one of the leading authorities on street drugs in the UK."

"What did he find?" Nikki asked, glancing at Monty.

"Very high levels of scopolamine and ayahuasca. Scopolamine has been used a truth drug. It gets people confused, disorientated, and they often speak the truth when interrogated. It was widely used by the KGB and CIA in the seventies. But ayahuasca is different. It's from the Amazon rainforest and is a potent hallucinogen. It can cause vivid visions from past memories, and generate a trance-like state in which the person becomes different entirely. It's actually a form of psychosis, and it lasts several hours."

"Bloody hell," Nikki said. "I've heard of ayahuasca. It's illegal in the UK, right?"

"Yes. But it is still used in shamanic rituals all over the world, and in the UK it's taken in organised retreats. There have been cases of ayahuasca poisoning and hospital admissions here. The drug has grown in use."

Dr Raman paused to catch her breath. "But we're not dealing with ayahuasca alone. Together with scopolamine, it becomes a potent hallucinogen and psychosis inducer."

"English, please, doc. What do you mean?"

"It can drive people crazy, basically. They start to believe in an alternative reality. They might think they can fly, for instance." Dr Raman's voice dropped as she realised the significance of her words. "Or they might think people are after them. All sorts of paranoia, and weird beliefs. Essentially, they become different people."

They were silent for a while. Monty held Nikki's eyes, then blinked. "How would this drug be made? Or given to people?"

"It would have to be in the form of a paste, or liquid. Ayahuasca is often drunk, but it can be sold as a paste as well. It's the same with scopolamine. They can be mixed together into a paste."

"What would it taste like?"

"I don't think they have a particular taste, to be honest. Rodney, the toxicologist, said they can be bland tasting. So, if someone was putting them into chocolates, or cakes, the person who took them would only taste the sweetness."

Dr Raman paused for a beat. "Hetty send me a forensics report about the chocolate residues found on Chloe's fingertips. She had eaten those chocolates the day of her death. Maybe just hours before because she hadn't washed her hands – hence the residues."

Nikki could feel her heart pumping faster. She looked up to see everyone riveted on Dr Raman's voice. They could all guess what was coming next.

The pathologist said, "The chocolate residues on Chloe's fingers also contained this chemical. Which means the chocolates she ate that day poisoned her."

Nikki's breath hitched. "We don't know where she got the chocolate from. Can you give us any idea from the chemical composition? Or maybe Hetty can?"

"I spoke to Hetty already. It looks homemade, given the absence of food stabilisers, and the E number additive chemicals. Apart from that, we have no other clues. It's easy to buy the ingredients at any supermarket."

"The wrappers belong to a company called Maxwell," Kristy explained, "but I can't find them anywhere. I've looked online and on Companies House."

"The chocolate maker could be creating them at one of these designer websites just for himself," Monty suggested.

There was silence for a while as they all pondered their own thoughts.

Nikki looked at the others. It was Monty who spoke again. "Where did Chloe go that day? She met up with Mark in the afternoon, but then she took the bus to Iffley."

Nish couldn't hide the excitement in his voice. "And she went to that market stall. Could she have got the chocolates from there?"

Dr Raman's metallic voice came from the loudspeaker. "That makes sense. After ingesting the substance, within an hour or two, the person would start getting paranoid visions.

"What about the postmortem?"

"On Chloe's body we found DNA matching with Mark Ofori. She didn't have any signs of sexual activity. There was alcohol and cocaine in her bloodstream, and the rest you know."

"Thanks doc, keep me posted."

"Sheila, not doc," Dr Raman said. "And yes, I will."

THIRTY-TWO

Fiona woke with a start. Confusion settled in – for a moment, she didn't recognise where she was. Clutching the bedsheet to her chin, she looked at the door. It seemed unfamiliar: green, with a coat hook. She could have sworn someone had been knocking, but now she realised it was just a dream. Nightmares of someone breaking into her house, kicking down the door, had filled her tormented night. She had barely got any sleep. She'd tossed and turned, eventually passing out at some point.

She looked around at the whitewashed walls and the books stacked on the shelves. Then she remembered. She had called Jemima, who hadn't answered, and then Sally. When no one returned her calls, she checked herself into a bed and breakfast in Botley.

She hadn't wanted to go home last night. She didn't feel safe – and she expected the police to call at any second. Mark had told her not to be afraid of that; that she had a good story.

She'd been foolish to be on the college grounds with Chloe the night before last. She clutched her head and fell back onto the bed. What was she thinking? There were bound to be cameras, and they had probably seen her and Chloe...

She should have gone away with Mark. But when she saw him the day before yesterday, he had been strange. Somehow aloof and distant. Despite what they had shared recently, she knew Mark was hiding something important.

She needed to get out of Oxford. But the train or bus wasn't safe – the police might be keeping an eye on the station. Then she remembered Sally had a car.

Fiona got ready quickly. She pulled a hoodie low over her face and put on dark sunglasses. She had to be extra vigilant.

When she reached Holywell Street, she abruptly stopped – she couldn't go any closer to New College. She sent Sally a text:

> My mum's ill. I need to go back home. Can you please give me a lift?

To her immense relief, Sally answered.

> Oh no. What's happened to your mum?

> She's been admitted to hospital with Covid. I'm really worried about her.

> Have the police been in touch?

> Yes, and I've spoken to them. They're treating Chloe's death as an accident. They know I'm going to see my mother.

It was a pack of lies, and Fiona waited with bated breath. After what seemed like an eternity, Sally replied.

> Okay. When do you want to go?

Fiona felt her body sag with relief.

> In one hour?

> Okay, that works. Let me tell the police I'm going to take you back to Cheltenham. Where shall we meet?

Fiona stared at the phone in disbelief. How stupid could this bitch be?

She thought of her options quickly. If she told Sally not to inform the police, Sally would be suspicious. And if Sally told the police, they'd know Fiona was trying to get away. She was doomed, in other words.

She should have thought of this before contacting Sally. Miss Goody Two-Shoes. More like Miss Dumb. Fiona swore in frustration. How we she going to get herself out of this?

> Actually, Sally, don't worry. I'm going to call my brother. Sorry, I forgot that I had a missed call from him. It's fine, okay?

> Are you sure?

> Yes, it's fine. Don't worry. I'll keep you posted.

Fiona walked away as fast as she could. She was hungry. She decided to go to Iffley, which had a market by the riverside. She'd enjoy stretching her legs in the sunshine. She needed some time to think. Getting out of Oxford would help.

As for Mark... if he didn't want to stay in touch, there wasn't much she could do about it.

She put her headphones on and walked along the riverside path to Iffley. At the market in Iffley, she picked up some snacks. She saw a charity stall with an old man behind the counter. He had a white beard and a kind face. His blue coat looked familiar, but she must be mistaken. She'd never seen him before.

Fiona bought a couple of cakes from him.

"Thank you so much," the man said, giving her some

change. "You remind me of someone. Have you been to this market before?"

"No," Fiona replied.

"Well" – the old man smiled – "you're my daughter's age. She used to study at Oxford. I might have you confused with one of her friends."

"Oh, I see."

"It's nice to be young, isn't it? You've got your whole life ahead of you."

"I guess so." Fiona smiled and turned to leave, but the old man stopped her.

"Here, take some of these chocolates. It's my bestseller. Give them to your friends."

Fiona declined, but the man insisted. He was kind, Fiona thought. She took the extra chocolates and left.

After a coffee and slice of the cake, she got on the bus back to Oxford. She unwrapped one of the chocolates and put them in her mouth. They were gorgeous. She had another – she wanted to treat herself after a hard day.

Walking around town, she didn't feel quite right. Her eyes felt heavy, and she wondered if she was coming down with the flu. She went to see her tutor, but he wasn't in.

People were staring at her. She started feeling anxious.

Fiona felt a tingling in her fingers, and her heart started pumping faster. The crowd of bodies in the street seemed to press against her. She retreated to a shopfront and leaned against the wall. The door behind her opened suddenly, making her jump. A man stepped out, looking at her strangely. He wore a blue coat. Fiona couldn't help thinking she knew him. He had a white beard and looked like the old man she'd just seen in Iffley. Then his face changed, and he appeared younger, with a black beard. The man stared at her curiously, then walked on.

She started to feel dizzy. Shards of sunlight were jagged knives all of a sudden, sending pinpricks into her skin. The noise on the street seemed to rise, assaulting her ears. A sharp whine came from somewhere. Her vision blurred, and she thought she might fall over. She steadied herself by leaning against the wall and opened her mouth to breathe.

As she tried to walk again, she saw the old man. He was standing across the road, and his white beard seemed longer now, with a black cap on his head. He crossed the street and headed toward her. What did he want? Panicked, Fiona started walking faster. But when she looked behind her, she couldn't see him anymore.

"She killed her friend." Two women were talking in whispers and pointing at her. "The police are coming to get her. They've got new evidence against her."

Fear surged in Fiona's heart. What was happening to her? Why were all these people against her? She walked back to her house as fast as she could. There was no one in the kitchen, and she ran up the stairs. The house was tall, with a loft-conversion on the third floor. Fiona went up to the loft and tried the door. It was locked. But there was a window that led out onto the roof.

She could still hear the bubble of voices from the street; it was as if she had carried them with her. She pressed her hands over her ears, but the voices continued. It felt like the entire street was talking about her. She needed to get away. Desperation took hold as she looked at the window. She yanked it open and climbed out onto the roof.

She stepped onto the flat roof and peered over the edge. Far below, she could see people milling about on the street. They didn't seem to pay any attention to her, until she saw someone looking up. It was the old man. He had taken off his black cap, and his white beard glinted in the sunlight. He was looking up at her, and a smile appeared on his face. It was an evil, knowing smile that made her shiver with fright. Then he crossed the road, heading for her house.

Fiona panicked. She had to get out of there as quickly as she could. The flat roof led to a tiled section, and then to another roof. If she could get over the slight incline, she could get to the roof of the other house. Fiona started to climb, but her foot slipped. Desperately, she tried to hold on to the tiles, but there was nothing to stop her fall.

She screamed in fear. Her right hand desperately tried to grab the gutters, but her nails ripped off, and she slipped down further. She howled in agony, her fingertips holding the guttering as it bent under her weight. Then that too buckled, giving way. A vortex of anguish wailed from her throat as she fell to the street below.

THIRTY-THREE

Nikki and Kristy were in Iffley market. They walked around but couldn't find the stall with the blue and white awning.

Kristy said, "The researchers rang all the farmers and businesses that have stalls here. Only a few have not replied. I'll call them back again today."

Nikki sighed as she looked around. "That stall has to be around somewhere. Even if the man's packed up for the day."

Chloe could've got the chocolate from anywhere. It had to be homemade, and she had already spoken to Chloe's father and stepmother. They didn't make chocolate at home, and Chloe hadn't been back home that recently. Jemima and Sally had also denied making chocolate. She couldn't help thinking the answer lay here, in Iffley market.

Kristy was speaking to a farmer, and she turned around. "This man remembers a new guy with a beard. He used to set up a stall at the end, three down from his."

Nikki walked up to the man, who was behind an array of cheese, and their accompanying strong smell at his stall table.

"Can you describe him?"

The man shrugged. "He was older, I'd say in his sixties. He

wore an old blue army coat and had a white beard. The stall was for an age-related charity. Not Age Concern but a different name. Can't remember it now. He was a chocolatier, I think."

Nikki and Kristy exchanged a glance. "Did you try any of his stuff?"

"Nope. He wasn't that busy to be honest. He wasn't here every weekend. Kept to himself, never spoke to anyone. I said hello once, that was it."

Nikki showed him a photo of Chloe. "Did you see this woman in the market?" They had shown the photo to several stall owners already and drawn a blank.

"No," the cheesemonger said. "Sorry." He looked Nikki and Kristy up and down. "What's this about? Has owt happened?"

"We need to find that old man without delay. If you see him, please call the police."

They walked off. Kristy was excited. "At least we know the stall was for an elderly person's charity. We should be able to find that business on our list."

Nikki's phone buzzed and so did her radio. As she twirled the black knob, she heard Kristy's radio also crackle to life.

"*IC1 female found injured in Cowley. Request all units to respond.*"

THIRTY-FOUR

The main road that went through Cowley was broad, but the side roads were narrow. Fiona lived in such a side road, which was now blocked with a police car and crime-scene tape. This was causing traffic chaos, cars honking, and Cowley's colourful residents being frank with their displeasure.

Nikki and Monty shouldered their way through the crowd that had gathered at the mouth of Fiona's street. A row of uniformed officers were doing their best to keep the aggrieved residents who wanted entry to their street at bay.

Inspector Hardy, a uniformed veteran of the Thames Valley Police, lifted the tape so Nikki and Monty could come through.

"We can't hold this lot for long," he shouted above the uproar. "How long do you need to hold the roadblock for?" Hardy asked.

"As soon as scene of crime is done, we can open it," Nikki said. "Have they arrived?"

"Yes, about ten minutes ago. Better tell them to hurry up. My guys can't hold them for too long."

Nikki and Monty put on shoe coverings, gloves and a mask,

signed their names and rank on the clipboard that the uniformed constable held out, and went inside the house.

The terraced house wasn't small, but it needed some decorating. The paint outside was old, and there was a patch of damp under the upstairs window.

On the left of the narrow hallway, the kitchen door was open and a scared young woman sat at the table. A female uniformed constable was standing in front of her, asking questions. She turned when Nikki came in.

"Please leave us," Nikki said, and the constable nodded. Monty shut the door. Nikki showed her card and introduced herself.

"Who are you?"

"Lucy Margot. I live here. There are two others, but they've left for home." Lucy's face was pale and drawn – Nikki didn't blame her.

"We're sorry about this," Nikki said. "But we won't be here long. Have you told your family?

"Yes, my parents are aware. My sister lives in Reading; she's coming down later to stay with me."

"Good. Can you please tell us when you last saw Fiona?"

"This morning. She came back from a friend's house party, she said. She looked tired. She had a bag with her, and a backpack. I thought she had packed a lot for a house party. Seemed like she had been somewhere else. Or was going somewhere."

Lucy spoke in a rush, and Nikki could tell she was nervous. "Did you ask her if she was off anywhere?"

"No. She went upstairs. I was in my room. I was back in the kitchen making lunch when I heard her leave. She didn't say goodbye."

"Did she have the bags with her again?"

"I'm not sure."

"And when did she come back?"

"Not that long after. Maybe a couple of hours? The front door slammed and she ran upstairs."

"And then?"

A new fear blossomed on Lucy's face. Tears glistened in her eyes. Then I heard a crash outside. It was loud, and nearby. I got up from the desk. I was in my room. I came downstairs, but it was quiet. I went in the garden, and that's when I heard the screaming outside. I went back through the house, and saw people had gathered on the street. That's when I saw..."

Tears rolled down her cheeks, and she wiped them. "There was so much blood. I could only recognise Fiona from her clothes and hair. She was lying face down... The ambulance came quickly. So did the police." She looked at Nikki, fear still alive in her eyes. "I've told them this already."

"Thank you," Monty said. Lucy turned to look at him. "When Fiona came back, and ran upstairs, do you think she went up to her room? Think carefully."

"Yes, because I heard her moving upstairs. But then she ran up again, into the loft – I heard her moving up there. There was a screeching sound, and I think that was the loft Velux window opening."

"And you're sure no one else came into the house? Was the back door locked?"

"Yes, we always keep the back door locked and our windows shut. Four women live here. Burglaries happen in Cowley. We're very careful."

"Thanks," Nikki said. "Can you show us Fiona's room, please?"

When they reached Fiona's door, Lucy excused herself and went to her room. Nikki opened the door with her gloved hand and they stepped inside. The room, though big, was messy, even for a typical student dig. Clothes lay on the floor, and some underwear was strewn on the bed.

Nikki went to the desk by the bay window and opened the

first drawer. She rifled through the papers, and stopped when she found a couple of chocolate wrappers. She turned to Monty.

Nikki held up one of the wrappers to the light. They were red and brown. The brand name was just visible, written in miniscule letters on the wrappers. "Maxwell. Both Chloe and Fiona ate the same chocolates." She frowned.

Why was this familiar to her?

She didn't know, but the maddening impulse that she was missing something kept circling in her mind. She was still thinking when her phone beeped with a text. It was her mother. She wanted to speak to Nikki, and had said it was urgent. Nikki called her back.

Clarissa said, "You told me to call if I remembered anything unusual. And I did notice something. I've noticed something weird. Or someone, to be precise. It's this old man. He's got a white beard, and he wears a long blue coat. I've seen him walk past the house a few times. He's got dark glasses on so I can't see his face."

A numbness slowly spread to Nikki's limbs. She felt unsteady. She pulled the desk chair, and sat down on it, heavily. The man's description matched what Jemima had described – the old man Chloe thought was following her in the nightclub.

"Do you recognise him?"

"No." Clarissa paused. "But I have to say, there's something oddly familiar about him. Maybe I've seen him at the AA meetings. Or around town. I don't know."

"Do not approach that man, okay? And you're moving in with me from today."

"What? I can't just up sticks like that!"

"Mum, listen to me. If he's the same person I'm thinking of, that man is dangerous. I'll explain why later when I see you. Lock your doors. Don't go out till I come around, okay?"

"You're getting me worried now. What on earth is going on?"

"Like I said, I'll tell you later. Pack your things. Stay there till I get there."

"What about Frodo?" Frodo was Clarissa's cat.

"Bring him and his food with you."

Clarissa sighed. "Alright. If you insist. What time will you get here?"

Nikki looked at her watch. "Give me a couple of hours. If it's any later, I'll let you know."

THIRTY-FIVE

Nikki went out into the street, where Inspector Hardy was speaking to an irate resident. Cars were honking on the main road, and shouts of annoyance floated over from the group beyond the crime-scene tape.

Monty hurried over to Nikki. He was speaking to a couple of the residents. "Uniforms have taken statements from the residents. Do you want to see where she fell?"

Nikki nodded, and they walked to the side of the house. More people had gathered, and Nikki groaned when she saw a small, prim woman in a well-pressed dress hurrying over to her. The woman had brown hair and hard, calculating eyes. Nikki knew she was a reporter before she opened her mouth.

"Geraldine Cuthbert from the *Oxford Herald*. You must be the detectives, am I correct?"

"No comment," Nikki said, trying to brush Geraldine off, but the woman was used to it and like a dog with a bone. She hurried along, practically running to keep up with Nikki's five foot nine frame.

"A second student has died in two days, in the same fashion.

Both fell to their deaths. They were both acting anxious and paranoid. What do you suspect, Detective?"

Nikki halted. Her eyes searched Geraldine's uncompromising face. "Who told you they were acting paranoid?"

"Sources," Geraldine answered primly. "Apparently, the students dabbled in narcotics as well."

"What sources?" Nikki demanded.

"You know the rules, Inspector. Are you an inspector, and SIO for this case? What's your name?"

"Come here." Nikki gestured to the side alley, opposite the house. She waved at Monty, who was closer to the white forensic tent erected over where Fiona had fallen. He nodded and went inside the tent.

When they were in the alley, Nikki got close to Geraldine. And closer, till the small woman was up against the wall. Nikki lowered her face till it was millimetres from Geraldine's. She could smell her cheap perfume and hairspray.

"Detective, what are you—"

"Shut up," Nikki hissed. "Where's your phone?"

"What?"

"Turn your phone off."

"But detective—"

Nikki prodded Geraldine's chest with a finger. "Do. It. Now."

Geraldine had turned pale. She took her phone out and did as she was told.

"Now," Nikki said, keeping the finger in the centre of Geraldine's chest, as if pinning her to the wall. The reporter looked scared, which pleased Nikki immensely.

"Either you tell me who your source was, or I blacklist you from any press conference Thames Valley Police ever holds again. No police officer will ever speak to you again."

"You can't do that. I can—"

"Shut up. I can, and I will. I'll call your editor right now. Shall I?"

Geraldine stared at Nikki, then realised she meant business. Her shoulders slumped. "Alright. A man called me just an hour ago. He said he had information on the girls who died. They were taking a new kind of drug. One that made them paranoid. The drug is now rife inside Oxford."

"Who is this man? Did he leave a name? How did he get your number?" The words left Nikki in a rush, her heart rate spiking upwards.

"He didn't give me his name. My number is easily available from the front desk of our office – I'm the crime reporter. He said he knew the girls and had seen what happened to them. He knows their friends."

"Did he talk about any other student specifically?"

"No. Just Chloe and Fiona."

Nikki thought quickly. The man knew what happened to Fiona as soon as she fell. Was he following her around?

Was this the same old man that Chloe used to visit at the market?

"Did he call from a withheld number?"

"Yes."

"What else did he tell you?"

"What I just said. He had information on more students he said, before hanging up."

Geraldine tried to stand straighter, and Nikki stepped back. Geraldine squared her shoulders, then looked at Nikki curiously.

"This man is important for you, right? What's his connection to the girls?"

Nikki closed her eyes and sighed. "The best you can do is keep quiet about this. The worst thing would be to write about it. It would also hamper our investigation and reduce our chances of finding the killer. Do you understand?"

Geraldine's coal black eyes glittered at Nikki. "If you don't want me to write about this, then give me something more."

Nikki stared at her grimly. "This isn't a negotiation. What did this guy sound like? Young, old, what sort of voice?"

Geraldine blinked. "An older man's voice. Not very deep. Quite raspy in fact."

"Any sounds in the background?"

The reporter's eyes crinkled. "Oh, yes. I could hear a beeping sound, then grating. As if he was somewhere gates were closing. But then I heard water running as well. I think he moved because I didn't hear the sounds later."

"Water? What do you mean?"

"Like when a boat passes by. That sort of sound."

Nikki narrowed her eyes. "So you think he was by the river?"

"It could be. Like I said, he moved away, and I couldn't hear those sounds anymore."

This man had an old guy's voice – or was he a smoker? They often sounded older than their years. Nikki couldn't jump to conclusions, but... Nikki knew she was missing something that was tantalisingly close to reach. It was maddening. Her brains jostled around, trying to look for the connection. It was there, in the jumble of detail, somewhere. A line that connected the dots.

She fixed Geraldine with a stare. "Thank you. Can I please ask you to keep quiet about this?"

"Why?" the woman asked, undaunted. "You think he's behind the girls' deaths, don't you?"

"It's possible," Nikki admitted. She had to give Geraldine something. She also knew what the reporter had heard in the background was important. She just needed to figure out why.

She gave Geraldine her card. The reporter whistled. "So. You're the famous Nikki Gill. The DI who cracked the historic sexual abuse gang in Oxford."

Nikki said nothing. "If you remember anything, call me."

Geraldine smoothed down her dress. "I could tell you the same thing, Inspector."

Inside the tent, it was stuffy and hot due to the glare of the halogen lights. A SOC technician was kneeling on the floor. The body was gone, and white chalk marks showed where Fiona had fallen. Blood had darkened some spots, circled in white.

"Any personal belongings?" Nikki asked. The SOC technician looked up and pulled down his mask. Nikki hadn't seen him before. She wondered where Hetty was.

"Nowt as yet," the man said in a northern accent. He had a short beard, and his blue eyes twinkled. "But we got her phone from her body, and purse. They're in the lab right now."

"Thanks."

Nikki and Monty left, and walked back to the car. Monty put his siren on, but it was still slow going through the traffic. Finally, after almost half an hour, they arrived at John Radcliffe Hospital.

THIRTY-SIX

The hospital room was hushed, the silence only broken by the soft beeps from the screen above the bed. Squiggly lines in red, yellow, and blue played across the monitor. Nikki didn't know much about them, but she could see that Fiona's oxygen levels were above 95%. Then she noticed the oxygen cannulas going into Fiona's nose. She turned to the white-coated doctor standing next to her. His name was Mark Saunders, a consultant in the intensive care unit.

"Can I speak to her?" Nikki whispered. She didn't hold out much hope. Her heart had sunk when she had first seen Fiona on the bed. The poor girl wasn't moving, her eyes closed, and her neck immobilised by a plastic brace. White bandages were wrapped around her head.

"I'm afraid not," Dr Saunders whispered back. "Her brain injury was severe, leading to massive intracranial haemorrhage – bleeding in the brain, basically. I'm surprised she's alive."

Nikki's breath hitched in her throat. She felt helpless and furious. She couldn't shake the feeling of responsibility. Fiona had slipped through her fingers, and she shouldn't have let that happen. Her instincts had been right. She had let Fiona down, and she couldn't forgive herself.

Dr Saunders said quietly, "Between you and me, I don't think she's going to survive. She's in a persistent vegetative state now, fully dependent on the breathing machine. But because she's young, we've kept her alive for now."

"Have her parents been informed?"

"They're on their way."

Nikki realised she wouldn't achieve anything by standing there. Remorse and rage mixed into a lethal cocktail in her heart and she felt like lashing out, hitting something – anything that would release this new confused charge of feelings. She exhaled softly. She couldn't let the frustration get to her. She thanked the doctor and walked out. Monty was standing outside. She glanced at him and shook her head. No words were necessary.

The double doors at the end of the ward opened, and a middle-aged couple hurried down. The woman had blonde hair and anxiety bulged in her eyes. Instinctively, Nikki knew they were Fiona's parents.

"Do you know where Fiona Bartlett is?" the woman asked. "I'm Sarah, her mother."

"She's in that room." Before she could say anything else, Sarah had rushed inside, followed by the man. Nikki wanted to say she needed to speak to them, but that would have to wait.

"What's the latest?" she asked Monty. He'd given her the details on their way down, but Nikki wanted an update.

"As you know uniforms were called by pedestrians and Fiona was brought here. They've now secured the area and started a door-to-door. Traffic is going through CCTV as we speak."

"Was anything found on her? Like a note?" Nikki raised her eyebrows.

"No." Monty shook his head. "Her clothes have been submitted to the scene of crime team. Hetty is aware and is treating it as a priority. A blood sample has already been sent to Dr Raman. The hospital will carry out their own checks."

Nikki clenched her fists. "It's all the same – Fiona fell to her death, just like Chloe."

The door opened, and the man emerged. "My name is John Bartlett," he said. He was in his sixties, with balding hair. "The doctor inside said you're the police, is that correct?"

Nikki nodded and showed her warrant card. Mr Bartlett's face was heavy with grief, his cheeks sagging, eyes red-rimmed. "What happened to my daughter?"

"We're not sure yet, but we're looking into what happened."

"This is not like her. She doesn't go climbing on roofs. Someone did this to her." Mr Bartlett's forehead contracted, and anger flickered in his eyes. "Can you tell me what happened?"

Nikki raised a hand to placate him. "I'm very sorry, Mr Bartlett, we are trying our best to piece everything together. Please give us some time to do so."

Mr Bartlett's face quivered, and his red-rimmed eyes were moist. "Find out who did this to my daughter. She wouldn't do this of her own accord."

"We will," Nikki said. Mr Bartlett's desolate, grief-laden eyes held her own, then he turned and went back into the room.

Nikki felt empty inside, her chest hollowed out. She wanted to slump into a chair and forget everything that was happening. Monty grabbed her elbow and steered her out of the ward. Inside the lifts, he put an arm around her shoulders and pulled her into a hug as her eyes misted. She couldn't forget Fiona's face as she lay there, looking so peaceful, and so... dead.

They left the hospital and walked to the car. Nikki stared down at her hands.

"Get a grip," Monty said. "We'll find whoever did this, okay?"

Nikki exhaled and clenched her fists. She dug the heels of

her hands into her eyes and dropped them. Slowly, the shock was dissipating, the tumult of emotions and adrenaline starting to fade.

"Let's get back to the nick," she whispered. "Let's see where Fiona went after getting back to her house this morning. There must be something on CCTV."

THIRTY-SEVEN

Mark's mouth went dry as he turned onto Marsh Road. Something was wrong. Terribly wrong. Police cars blocked the street where Fiona lived, their blue lights painting the Victorian terraces in ghostly pulses.

His phone felt heavy in his pocket – Fiona's last message from a few hours ago still unanswered:

> Please come. I need to tell you something important.

Now, watching unmarked police vehicles and officers in tactical gear surrounding her house, those words took on a darker meaning.

The bitter taste of adrenaline flooded his mouth as he backed away slowly, trying to look casual. His heart wasn't just racing – it was trying to punch through his ribcage. Why were they here? What did they know? The questions ricocheted through his mind like stray bullets.

He saw a man in a suit stepping out of Fiona's front gate. He looked around him, and then their eyes met across the street. Mark was too late to turn away. He knew he had been spotted.

"You!" The detective's shout cut through the murmur of radio chatter. "Stop right there!"

Mark's body moved before his mind could catch up, spinning him around toward Between Towns Road. The sound of heavy footsteps behind him sent fresh panic coursing through his veins. He pushed through a group of onlookers gathered at the street corner, ignoring their startled protests.

His trainers slapped against the pavement as he sprinted past the betting shop, his reflection fragmenting across its darkened windows. The street ahead was crowded with the usual mix of students and locals, most heading toward Cowley Road's evening attractions.

"Police! Make way!" a voice boomed behind him.

Mark ran as fast as he could. The surge of people forced him to slow momentarily, and panic clawed at his throat.

The Templars Square shopping centre offered temporary shelter. Mark crashed through the automatic doors, nearly colliding with a security guard. The fluorescent lights overhead made him feel exposed, vulnerable. Every face he passed now could be used as a witness for the police. His vision tunnelled, black edges creeping in. Not now. He couldn't afford a panic attack now.

He burst out onto Barns Road, gasping for air. Sweat ran into his eyes and his shirt clung to his back like a second skin. The partially demolished Temple Cowley Pools complex loomed ahead – a maze of construction equipment and shadowed corners. Mark spotted a gap in the security fence and squeezed through, feeling wire catch and tear at his clothes.

Mark's mind raced faster than his feet. Fiona's message, the police presence, it was all connected, but how? What had she been trying to tell him? The questions pounded in his head with each frantic heartbeat.

He scrambled through the skeletal remains of the pool building, darkness gathering in its concrete corners. His foot caught on a piece of debris, sending him sprawling. Pain shot through his palms as they scraped against rough concrete. Mark rolled over, chest heaving, staring up at the exposed beams above. For a moment, the world spun around him. He tried to get up, but he heard pounding steps and then a body crashed into him, pushing him down.

More officers appeared, rough hands securing his wrists with handcuffs that bit into his flesh. He was hauled up by the neck. Then they took him outside.

Mark could now see the detective's face. "I'm DI Monty Sen. You're Mark Ofori, right?"

He nodded in silence. There was no point in lying. The game was up. But he needed to know. He looked at Monty.

"What happened to Fiona?" Monty didn't answer and walked away but Mark pushed himself forward, against the grip of the constable restraining him. Monty stopped.

"I need to know," Mark shouted. "Why are the police here? What happened to her?"

Monty stepped closer. He lowered his face to Mark's level. "You don't know?"

"No." Mark glared at him. "Why would I be asking you if I did?"

Monty cocked his head to one side. "I guess you also don't know what happened to Chloe?"

Mark paled. "What's happened to Chloe?"

Monty looked at him without responding, then turned away. Mark tried to move, but this time two burly constables held him in check.

"You need to tell me," Mark shouted.

Monty turned at that. "Why? You're under arrest. I don't have to tell you anything, but anything you do say can be taken as evidence."

"Well, you can use this," Mark spat out. "I work for MI5. My number is CX 3461. I repeat, CX 3461. I'm an undercover agent."

THIRTY-EIGHT

"One year's worth of undercover surveillance!" Dean Patmore bellowed, flinging the folder across the room, the highly confidential papers flying. "Do you know how much flack I'm going to get for this? The Chief Constable has called already. They're going to crucify us. No, not you. Me!"

Nikki and Monty were in an emergency meeting with their Detective Superintendent after Mark Ofori's surprise revelation.

Patmore got up and opened the window. He lit up a cigarette, then blew smoke out. Monty glanced at Nikki, foreboding in his eyes.

Patmore clutched the windowsill and smoked, his back to them. He then slapped the windowsill with his free hand, and the window shuddered. Nikki knew it was best to hold her silence, for now. Let the storm blow over.

Patmore stubbed his cigarette on the window frame and threw it out, instead of putting the stub in the ashtray on the table. He turned and walked up to Nikki and Monty, who remained standing quietly.

"What do you want me to tell them, eh? That we were

investigating an accident, and caught some kids doing drugs? And that's why we blew up a multi-million-pound operation?"

Patmore looked in pain, like he was being dragged out of water by a fishhook in his nose. The man didn't take stress well. If the situation wasn't so dire, Nikki might have found it comical.

"The surveillance on the OCN was gathering pace. Mark was getting close to the leaders of the OCN. How could an accident make you investigate Mark so intently?"

Nikki stiffened. "Not just an accident, sir. Two young women have died in identical fashion. I just heard from Hetty – Fiona also had chocolate stains on her fingers. It's possible both girls were poisoned."

"And what was Mark's connection to them?"

"I think he was romantically involved with both of them. He was also buying drugs from the Botley Boys Gang, acting as a dealer."

Patmore threw his cigarette out and turned slowly. "MI5 have briefed me. Mark was gathering intel on the gang. Done well, that lad. Given a few more weeks, or months, he would've got evidence against all of them. He was wearing a wire every time he met the gang members."

Nikki sighed in frustration. She had been part of such operations before – but never with MI5. She knew they had their own rules. They wanted intelligence from the police but didn't necessarily share what they found.

Patmore collapsed on his chair and massaged his forehead. "This was a joint forces op with the NCA and MI5. I now need to justify what happened." He glared at Nikki. "You're the SIO. You need to do the report."

"I already have, sir. If Mark had not avoided us and had cooperated in our investigation, none of this would've happened. He got spooked when the police contacted him. There was no need for that. He's an inexperienced undercover agent, sir. He could've answered our questions and moved on."

Nikki's words seem to cut through the angry haze in Patmore's mind. His forehead contracted, and his eyes became slits.

"Do you still suspect him of murdering that girl?"

"I haven't spoken to him yet. But he wasn't on the college grounds, according to the witnesses and CCTV. He could've found another way, but no intruder into the college was seen on CCTV on the third of June."

Patmore grunted and reached for the cigarette packet. Then he swore and moved his hand away.

"Let him go. I don't want any more hassle."

"But I need to question him first, sir," Nikki said quickly. "He remains a suspect."

"I don't think so." Patmore frowned. "But okay, question him, then let him go. I don't want any more bollocks from MI5."

THIRTY-NINE

Mark was waiting for them in the interview rooms upstairs, and Nikki and Monty made their way to Room 4. These rooms were nicer, with carpets instead of the hard lino floors, and flowers on the table by the sofa.

Mark had rejected the offer of a solicitor. It wasn't necessary as he wasn't under arrest anymore. But Mark could still have a solicitor if he wanted. After all, they were dealing with a double murder case now.

Nikki knocked on the door and entered. Mark stood up from the sofa.

He was tall and handsome, and she could see why the girls liked him. His dark eyes glinted at her. He didn't seem angry. His face was impassive, his posture straight and dignified. Nikki could immediately see he wasn't a common drug dealer. He wore a blue polo neck and jeans, but even in his casual clothing, he had the bearing befitting a man of substance. He also looked older than his twenty-one years.

"Hello Mark," she said. "Nice to meet you."

"Pleasure is all mine," he replied. Nikki saw a trace of irony in the light tug of his lips. It faded quickly. Nikki could see the grief in his eyes, and in the slump of his shoulders.

"Is it true?" he whispered. "Both Chloe and Fiona are dead?" He looked at Monty, who nodded briefly.

"Yes, unfortunately. Both died in the same way. Poisoned, we believe."

"Mark," Nikki said, "were you avoiding us to protect your undercover status?"

"Yes. I couldn't afford to blow it. I was instructed by my handler to avoid contact with you guys, even if it meant going dark. That's what I did."

Nikki watched him. He was relaxed and his body language and facial expressions didn't suggest he was lying.

"Why did you come back to Cowley?"

"Fiona sent me a text on my burner phone. She had something to share before she went home. Something important." Mark's eyes flickered down and he gripped his hands together. "I didn't know about Chloe."

"You saw her the night she died. In fact, you were the last known person to see her."

Mark looked up. "She'd been going to Iffley to meet a man her mother knew. She thought he might know what happened to her mother. She had been focused on that over the last few weeks."

Nikki and Monty exchanged a glance.

"Can you explain more?" Monty asked.

"We went to her house, and she wanted to show me her mother's stuff. Then she said there was a box in the attic. We went up there and she found a diary, which she hadn't seen before, inside the box. She studied the diary but never told me what was in it." Mark spread his hands. "The only thing I knew was that she found this man's name in the diary."

"What was the name?"

"She didn't tell me. All I knew was that she looked for this man and found him in Iffley. I should've taken more of an interest in it. I know her mother disappeared." Mark sighed, and the regret rippled across his face. "She wanted to do this on her own. Do you think this man had something to do with her death?"

Monty looked at Nikki, and she inclined her head. Monty said, "We think this man is elderly, but still very able physically. He ran a stall in Iffley market, a charity. It sold chocolates and confectionery. Have you been there with Chloe?"

"No, she went there alone. I never saw this guy."

"What happened to the diary?" Nikki asked. "We didn't find it on her, or in her belongings. Neither did we find her phone, or keys."

Mark stared at Nikki, then his eyes dilated as if a memory struck him. "She had the diary on her that last time we met. I remember seeing it sticking out of her pocket. I told her, and she said she wanted to have it when she saw the man."

Nikki and Monty were silent, staring at Mark. Monty said, "So there's a chance the man took the diary. But I don't think Chloe would just hand it over."

"No. She guarded that diary with her life," Mark said. "Did you ask her parents? Dad and stepmother, I mean."

"Yes, we did. They don't know, either. What was happening between you and Fiona?"

Mark's eyes flickered, and a shadow passed over him. "Fi and I had an affair. I'm not proud of it. Chloe didn't know." His hands massaged his forehead.

Nikki thought about the note in Chloe's pocket and the intruder at her home. "Did Chloe ever mention me?"

Mark looked up, startled. "You, as in, by name?"

"Yes."

His eyebrows creased together. "No. She was never in any trouble with the police. Why would she be?"

Nikki didn't think Mark was lying. So the person who left

the note, implicating her, was someone else. Chloe's killer, no doubt. Someone who had access to her either before, or just after her death.

She stared at Mark for a few seconds. "So. This was all an elaborate deception."

"If that's what you want to call it," Mark said.

"Tell me what happened on the third of June when you met Chloe."

Mark shrugged. "We met up after classes. There's a bar by the river next to Magdalene College. We met there for a drink."

"And then you walked into Cowley. Where did you go?"

"To see a couple of our friends. I dropped off a few packets, picked up some cash. I was feeding that cash back to Paul Diggins, one of the senior members of the Botley Road Gang."

"And then?"

"Chloe had to meet this man in Iffley."

"When did you see Chloe after that?"

"Later that evening, I saw her at the nightclub called Cargo. She wasn't in a good mood. I asked her what was wrong, but she wouldn't tell me. She was acting strange in fact." Mark lapsed into silence, his eyes narrowing as if he remembered something.

"What do you mean?"

Mark looked up at Nikki. "She was very paranoid. She said twice: 'He's after me.' I asked her who she meant, but she wouldn't tell me. She also said, 'You're all traitors.' And then she went away. I caught up with her a few times in the nightclub, but she didn't want to talk."

Alarms bells were ringing in Nikki's mind.

"What happened after that?" Monty asked.

"She left the nightclub I think – I couldn't find her. So I went out and rang her but she wouldn't answer. Then I went home."

Monty asked, "You don't think she was having a bad trip as she was high on drugs?"

Mark shook his head firmly. "No. We don't take drugs that can cause... paranoia. Something else was wrong with her."

"Could she have taken another substance?" Nikki asked. "One that made her paranoid, or threatened?"

"Yes, it's possible. I wanted to speak to her about it. But I couldn't find her."

Nikki was deep in thought. "How much did you tell Chloe about your undercover operation?"

"Nothing. She didn't know. I was just dealing as far as she knew. I didn't introduce her to Paul, or anyone else."

If Mark was speaking the truth, then he had no motive to kill Chloe. Nikki stared at him, trying to decipher the workings of his mind. He held her gaze, aware this was an important moment.

They were silent for a while. Nikki asked, "What did you think of Chloe's parents – Jeffrey and Angela?"

Mark shrugged. "Nothing out of the ordinary. I don't think Angela liked me much, but Jeffrey was alright."

"Why didn't Angela like you?"

Mark spread his hands. "You need to ask her that. I've got nothing against her. I didn't really care, as I was there for Chloe."

"Did Chloe tell you anything specific about her mother?"

"She missed her, in as much you can miss someone you never knew." Mark paused, and a veil seemed to pass over his face, darkening his expression. "But after she met this man, who knew her mother, she did say her mother wasn't at peace. She used the present tense."

"The present tense? As in, she's alive?"

"No, I don't think so. She meant her mother's spirit."

After a silence, Monty spoke. "She met this guy in Iffley. Do you know the address, or did you ever take her there?"

"No, sorry. She always took the bus."

FORTY

"We've got more CCTV of Chloe from Traffic," Nish exclaimed.

Nikki walked over to his desk, and Kristy joined them. On the screen, they saw the image of Chloe walking down a busy street.

It was the same images from before, showing Chloe in the Iffley market.

"Too many dark spots in Iffley," Nish said. "They can't find her after that."

Nikki couldn't hide her frustration. "Damn it. Where does she go after?"

Nish played the film again, and they watched as Chloe got on the bus. She went back to Oxford, into Hollywell Street and took the back entrance into New College.

"Where else does she go?" Nikki asked.

"To the gym, to the library, and her lectures at the university. She meets up with Mark and her friends several times. We've not found her with this old man."

"Check new arrivals into Iffley. Needle in a haystack, I know, but we need to check. The council might have new registries, and check utility companies for bills. Iffley doesn't have a police station, does it?"

"Nope."

Kristy ran out of the office, phone clutched to her ear. Nikki sat down next to Nish and Monty, who were checking new CCTV footage from today. The image showed a woman walking down Cowley High Street. Like before, Traffic had circled her in red. Nikki recognised Fiona. "This is three and a half hours ago," Nish said, pointing to the time and date stamp on the top right of the screen. He pressed play.

They watched as Fiona got on a bus numbered 43. Nish breathed softly. "That's the bus that goes to Iffley."

Nish was right. Fiona got off one stop away from Iffley. She crossed the road, walked down a path, then descended a small hill and disappeared from view. Monty said, "That's the Cherwell towpath..."

He sped up the tape, and after twenty minutes, they caught up with Fiona again. She was on the High Street, at Iffley market.

They watched as Fiona went inside a stall and came out. She did some food shopping, then took a side road where she vanished from sight again. "She might well be on the towpath," Nish said. They caught up with Fiona when she appeared at the bus stop again. She didn't go back to Cowley. She got off in central Oxford, then walked to All Souls College. "She probably went to see her tutor," Monty said.

They watched as Fiona came out of the college after five minutes. She walked to the bus stop and went back to Cowley. Nikki noted her movements started to become erratic now.

Fiona moved in and out of shops quickly. She came out of a store, then stopped dead in front of a man and shrank backwards. The man walked inside the store, ignoring her. Fiona went into a side alley and emerged a few minutes later. It wasn't easy to tell her facial expression from the CCTV image, but

Nikki thought she looked shaken. Fiona walked faster, crossing the road several times, looking over her shoulder.

"Was someone after her..." Nish murmured.

Cowley High Street was busy, as usual. "I can't see anything obvious," Monty said, his eyes scanning the four boxes on the screen. Each one showed Fiona from a different angle.

They tracked her until she turned left to enter her street, went inside a house and shut the door.

"Go back," Nikki instructed. "I want to see the High Street just as she went inside." Fiona wasn't visible on the screen anymore, but they saw people and cars moving on the High Street. Traffic lights flickered, cars stopped, and people crossed.

"There," Nikki said suddenly, thrusting a finger at the screen. Nish froze the image.

"What?" he said. "I can only see... Oh, yes!" He leaned closer, with Monty. "Do you mean that bearded man leaning against the railings by the zebra crossing, just outside the supermarket" Nish asked.

"He's elderly and wearing a blue coat. He's also got glasses on. But we can't jump to conclusions. There could be a number of men matching that description in Cowley at that time."

Nikki looked at Monty askance. "At exactly the same time as Fiona happens to cross the road, and looking in her direction? I'd say the chances aren't that high.

"Track him. Let's see what he does," Nikki ordered Nish.

The man stood still and watched as Fiona turned left. He turned his back and slowly walked down the street. He turned left, then entered Fiona's road. He emerged a few minutes later, moved at a leisurely pace down the High Street, and waited at the bus stop.

They watched as he got on the bus to Iffley. Nish rewound the film and zoomed into the man's face. The glasses were thick and the beard long. For some reason, the man looked familiar to Nikki.

"Have you seen him before?" she asked the others. Both men shook their heads. Nikki stared at the man on the screen, an odd suspicion nibbling away inside her. "I think that might be him," Nikki breathed, adrenaline spiking in her blood. "Get facial recognition on him and see if we find a match on the databases. I want him tracked, and every move followed."

Nish stood. "I'll go up to Traffic now."

FORTY-ONE

Nish burst in through the door, his eyes shining. He put his laptop on Nikki's table and opened it. "We got him at the stall, guv. The old man."

They watched as the screen showed Fiona walking around the market in Iffley. She went into a stall, and emerged a few minutes later. She adjusted the strap of the bag on her shoulders, then walked off. Instead of following her, now the camera stayed on the high street. Nish fast-forwarded the film.

Then they saw him. The old, bearded man with glasses. He had a bag on his shoulders and he closed the stall awning. Then he walked away, towards the bus stop. He got on the bus to Cowley, and they found him again on Cowley High Street, standing opposite as Fiona crossed it.

"What about the morning? Where was he?"

Nish sighed. "That's the problem. We can see him coming into the high street and setting up the stall for the market, but Traffic thinks he's used the backroads of Iffley – all the dark spots. We don't actually see him till he's two streets down from the high street."

"Show me," Nikki demanded.

As Nikki watched the man, that odd feeling of recognition surfaced again. It wasn't so much his appearance as the way he held himself: his gait.

"Where is he coming from?" Monty asked. "He clearly lives in Iffley and drives a car. How did he carry the gear to set up the stall?"

Nish shut down the film and clicked on another file, which showed the man going into a side street. They could see Iffley's church spire from there, but the street didn't have CCTV cameras. The man appeared from the street, crossing into the main avenue, carrying a big backpack and equipment on his shoulders.

"You know" – Monty frowned – "I don't think this man is as old as we think he is. He could be in disguise."

"I was thinking that..." Nikki said. "He goes in and out of that street a lot, carrying stuff into the market. He's pretty fit for an old man."

"Some people look old if they're sunburnt and have beards," Nish said.

"Look how he looks at the streetlights. He's trying to figure out where the cameras are," Nikki commented. The cameras tracked the man going into the market. "Go back," Nikki said. "Where was he before this?"

"We don't know guv." Nish looked apologetic. "He goes in and out of Iffley, and Traffic can't see him. Facial recognition picks him up in Cowley. But to be honest, we don't know where he is now. He can't be seen anywhere. It's like he went back to Iffley after Fiona's death, then vanished into thin air."

"How can that be? Is he hiding somewhere in Iffley?"

"Hang on." Monty's eyes were suddenly attentive. "Freeze the image." Nish did so. The screen showed the man at the mouth of the side street. He was about to cross the road. His hand was in his pocket.

"Play it in slow motion," Monty said. They watched him pull something out of his pocket, look at it, then shove it back in.

"It's a set of keys," Monty said. "That looks like a set of house keys to me, not car. He could be living on that street that has no cameras."

"That's right," Nikki exclaimed. "That's why he keeps going there. And we can see the church spire in the background. It can't be far from the church. Nish, can you get the street name?"

"We have to look at the various angles, but Traffic will be able to do it much quicker."

"Do that, now," Nikki said. She snatched up the phone on her desk and called Patmore. "Sir, I need permission to shut down all road exits to Iffley. I think our suspect is there. He's living on a street that's in a CCTV dark spot. Just for today, sir. We can reassess at first light tomorrow."

Nikki put the phone down. Monty was playing around with the map on the screen, focusing on Iffley.

"That street isn't far from the church. And the high street isn't far from Iffley Lock."

A buzzing sound suddenly grew loud in Nikki's ear, and then a brilliant flash of light, like an old bulb exploding, blinded her. She blinked, unable to see. Then she stared down at Monty, who was still unaware of her reaction.

"What did you say?"

He looked up at her, then raised his eyebrows. "The high street. It's close to Iffley Lock."

Iffley Lock.

Geraldine, the reporter, had heard a whistle and the sound of rushing water in the background. Nikki knew what that sound could be. When she was young, a friend's dad had a boat. Every time they went through a lock, the gates made that sound. She had been confused when Geraldine told her, but now the memory came flooding back.

The background noise Geraldine heard had to be the river lock, closing its gates. Iffley Lock.

"He's by the lock. That's how he travels. By the river."

"How do you know?"

"Because Geraldine, the reporter told me." Breathlessly, Nikki told him. "Shutting down the roads won't help. He might well have got away on a boat."

"But we saw him taking the bus back to Iffley. You mean after that?"

"Yes. I think he's already gone. Call the River Police." Nikki ran out of the door. "I'm going to talk to Patmore to activate the search boats."

FORTY-TWO

Clarissa was busy getting ready when she heard the doorbell ring. She was flustered, packing her clothes, as well as stuff for the cat, Frodo, who was on the bed, sniffing around the suitcase. The doorbell went again, and Clarissa huffed, then went downstairs.

She looked through the keyhole before she opened the door. A man had his back to the door. His hair was white, and he wore a dark grey jacket.

She opened the door a fraction, and the man turned. He was old, probably in his late sixties or early seventies. A few days' worth of light stubble rested on his cheeks. His slate grey eyes stared at her avidly, and a memory jolted in Clarissa's mind, then her heartbeat quickened. It couldn't be. Or could it? Her heart recognised this man, but her mind refused to accept it.

He read the look in her eyes, and a smile appeared on his face. "Yes," he said softly. "It's me. Hello Clarissa."

Clarissa put a hand over her chest, as if to quieten her restless heart. "Steven? Is that really you?"

His smile was sad, laced with regret. She saw a kindness in his face, an allowance to let bygones be bygones.

"Yes, it is. I moved back here with Wendy a few months ago. My mother passed away."

Old ghosts were jostling around in Clarissa's mind; long shut doors were creaking open.

"Your mother lived in Iffley."

"Yes, correct. You remember." He smiled again, and this time, his eyes glowed.

"I see." Clarissa leaned against the wall for support. She didn't know what to say or do. Then the urgent question surfaced in her brain. "What are you doing here?"

"I use this route often to get to New College. I've got a job there as the groundsman. I saw you one day on the street, and I saw where you lived." He sighed. "I hope you don't mind. I wanted to let bygones be bygones. You can't live looking behind with regrets, can you? So I thought I'd knock on your door."

Clarissa was still lost for words. Frodo appeared, brushing past her legs. He stood on the doormat, looking up at the stranger. His tail swayed: he didn't look happy.

"Where have you been all these years? I mean..." Clarissa touched her forehead, then brushed back hairs. "This is all so sudden."

"I know, and I'm sorry. Look, I can see this is causing you stress. Maybe this wasn't a good idea after all. I'll leave, shall I?"

Clarissa was still processing the facts. "How long have you worked in New College?"

"Four months. I moved back into Iffley about six months ago. I was meaning to get in touch with you, but Mum was unwell, and then she passed away, so I was busy with all of that." Steven pressed his lips together, and he looked uncertain. "I also wasn't sure if you'd want to meet me." He looked down, and a troubled expression marred his face.

"I'm sorry about what happened between us, obviously. I know it was a long time ago."

Clarissa nodded, the cloud of memories settling on her shoulders. Steven Pugh was Tommy's father. Her tragic son, Tommy, who passed away at such a young age. She had let Steven know. He hadn't responded to her call. There had been no funeral for Tommy, and she had not seen Steven for decades.

"And mostly," Steven said, his eyes heavy with sorry, "I'm sorry about what happened to Tommy. I was messed up then as well. But look..." He stood straighter, and squared his shoulders. "I turned my life around. I worked as a painter decorator for years, got a good business going, and also got married and settled down. Here's my wife and kid, look. Brian's now twenty-four, and he's studying law at Nottingham University."

He showed her the photo of a woman and a man on his phone. The man was clearly the son, he had his arms around the woman and they were smiling.

"That's Wendy, my wife," Steven said. "And Brian obviously. He's a good lad." The pride in Steven's voice was unmistakable.

Clarissa handed the phone back to him. She stared at Steven's smiling face. He was a different man, clearly.

"I've been living in Nottingham all these years, as that's where Wendy is from. But now I'm back and Wendy will join me shortly. She likes Iffley. She's been several times, to see Mum. Wendy wants to live here. And I grew up here, so it made sense."

Clarissa nodded. "I guess you caught me at a bad time. I'm actually moving in with my daughter Nikki for a few days."

Steven raised his eyebrows. "Oh, really? That'll be nice, I guess."

"Kind of. She's worried about me. Someone's been sending me weird messages. Nikki says it's for my own safety. She works for the police, you see."

"Ah, right. Well, you can't blame her for being worried." Steven smiled. "Good to see you anyway. I hope we can stay in touch."

"Maybe, yes." Clarissa said. She also wanted to let bygones be bygones.

Steven asked, "You said you needed to move to your daughter's. Do you need a lift? Or a hand with moving?"

Clarissa hesitated. Nikki had told her to stay in the house, but what if she could actually go to Nikki's? Wouldn't that be easier for Nikki? She was busy and sounded stressed on the phone.

"Actually, yes. Can you just hold on for a moment?"

"Sure. Take your time."

She shut the door and called Nikki. She didn't answer. Clarissa tried twice, then left a message. She was feeling more relaxed about Steven now. The doubts remained in her mind, but frankly, as Nikki often told her, she was too anxious about everything. Always checking she'd locked the doors ten times when she left the house and at night. Clarissa had been on tablets for her anxiety in the past. She didn't want it to get the better of her this time as well. And yet she felt the need to be cautious.

Clarissa felt easier. She went upstairs and dragged her suitcase down. It wasn't too heavy but it was still an effort. She opened the door and saw Steven standing outside the front gate. She called him and then asked him to put the suitcase in the car.

"Of course, no problem."

"Anything else?" Steven asked after putting the suitcase in his black Ford Focus.

"No, it's just me and the cat. I've got a cage for him, actually. Would you mind taking that, please?"

"Yes, sure."

Steven followed Clarissa into the house. She coaxed Frodo

into the cage, which he wasn't happy about at all. Frodo eventually went in, looking very grumpy.

Steven took the cage and then pointed at her coat. "Shall I take that as well?"

"Okay," Clarissa said. "I've got a small backpack upstairs. I'll get that and lock up. Then I'll see you in the car?"

"Yes, of course."

Clarissa went back up and slung the backpack over her shoulder as she headed downstairs. She patted her pockets, and realised she didn't have her phone. Then she remembered her phone was in her coat pocket – and Steven had already taken it.

She shut the door and turned the alarm on. That had been one of Nikki's ideas. So much for Nikki not being paranoid, Clarissa thought with a smirk. Nikki was more like her mother than she liked to accept.

Steven smiled and held the rear passenger door open for her. Clarissa thanked him and got in.

She looked around the car. It looked like an ordinary vehicle.

Steven was driving fast, as if he was in a rush to get her to Nikki's house. She looked at him, but his eyes were focused on the road. His knuckles were white on the steering wheel.

"Where's my coat?" she asked, not finding it on the seat.

"Oh, here it is." Steven slowed a fraction and gave Clarissa her coat. She patted through the pockets but couldn't find her phone. She also didn't have her purse. She frowned.

"Steven? I had my phone and purse in here. Has it dropped out on the front seat?"

He didn't answer at first, then she saw his hand roam over the seat once. He glanced in the wing mirror. His eyes were suddenly cold and watchful. The previous warmth she had seen was now absent.

"No." He increased the speed and overtook a couple of cars who honked at him. He beat the traffic lights, and then took the road towards Botley. Clarissa frowned.

"Why are you going towards Botley? Nikki lives in Kidlington. It's the other way."

Steven didn't answer. Clarissa checked the door. It was locked, and she couldn't wind her window down. Fear erupted in her heart, lashing against her spine.

"Steven? Stop the car!" Clarissa raised her voice. He remained silent, staring forward, his face carved in granite.

FORTY-THREE

Nikki knocked on Patmore's office door to find it open. Patmore was on the phone, and he waved her in. Nikki waved her hands through the air, trying to dispel the cigarette fumes, and shut the door reluctantly. Patmore put the phone down and shook out another cigarette.

Thankfully, the window was open. Patmore lit another cigarette and took a deep drag. "So, you think this old man in Iffley poisoned the students?"

"Yes, sir. Thanks for alerting the Gold Command. The roadblocks are in place and the river police are at the lock, checking the boats. I'm worried that he's already escaped."

"Iffley isn't that big. We should be able to find him. However, a lockdown on the roads will cause a massive jam, and a nightmare for traffic wardens." He turned to Nikki, smoke curling up from the cigarette between his fingers. "Have you got units dispatched to the suspect's potential address?"

"Yes, and I'm going to head there now. We can't let this man slip through our fingers. We're dealing with a nightmare as you can imagine. God knows how many people this man has poisoned now. Hopefully not all of them have the same reaction."

"Have you informed Public Health?"

"Yes – and the colleges also know. We've also put out alerts to all national supermarket chains just in case these chocolates ended up on their shelves – which I strongly doubt. This man was selling them at his market stall. He wasn't a big trader by any means."

"We can't keep Iffley under lockdown for long. You better get cracking."

It was late afternoon when Nikki arrived at Iffley High Street with Monty. The shops were closing up and people stood around, watching the police as they went through the market stalls. Farmers who'd set up the stalls protested as their wares were swabbed and, for some unfortunate cake and confectionary makers, confiscated.

Blue and white crime-scene tape barricaded the stall that belonged to the old man. There was no sign on top, and the stall was empty, the shelves bare. A long collapsible table stood in one corner, its legs folded. A white Tyvek-suit-wearing forensic officer was bent low at the waist, taking photos. Nikki recognised Hetty. She patted her on the back and the woman straightened. She pulled her mask down.

"You're keeping us on our toes, that's for sure," Hetty said. "What about the girl? She's in hospital, right?"

"Yes. It doesn't look good. How's it looking here?"

Hetty grimaced. "Rather innocuous to be honest. What you see is what we found. Nothing's been disturbed. I found some brown fragments on the ground. Look like they could be chocolate. I've taken samples and Dr Raman has some already. She should have an answer for us soon."

Hetty pointed to the shelf and the brush now in her hand.

"There must be fingerprints here. And after I run the digital image analyser of the forensic photos, I might find more material. So, an old man with a beard ran this stall, correct?"

"Yes. That's who we saw going in and out of the stall, setting it up, and following Fiona around. But we don't know who he is, yet. He's been clever, keeping to the dark spots in Iffley."

"Good luck finding him. If he's distributing these poisoned chocolates, let's just hope the rot's not spread too far."

"The colleges and Public Health are aware now. If you see those Maxwell wrappers, make sure you don't eat them."

"And I love a little chocolate, as you know." Hetty's chubby cheeks split into a grin.

"We found a boat owner by the lock whom you might want to speak to." Kristy rushed into the tent. "He says he saw a white bearded man walking up and down the canal this morning speaking on the phone. By the lock."

A uniformed constable nodded at Nikki and Kristy as they arrived by a row of houseboats tethered along the canal. He climbed onto the first houseboat and knocked on the door. Nikki saw movement inside through the glass windows. Then the door opened and a man stepped out, blinking in the sunshine and rubbing his eyes, as if he had been sleeping. As Nikki got closer, she detected the smell of cannabis. She wondered how much they could trust him. He seemed wary of them, staying in front of his open door.

Nikki showed her warrant card and introduced herself and Kristy. "When did you see the old man with the white beard?" she asked.

The man scratched the back of his neck. White dandruff fell from his scalp and settled on his shoulders. "About three hours ago?" He sounded vague. "Around two p.m. I saw him walking up and down, just outside my boat. People normally walk in one direction. He was having a conversation with someone. Then he walked away."

"Can you describe him in more detail?" Nikki pressed.

The man grimaced, blinking. "He was in his sixties or seventies, I'd say. White beard ran down to his chest. He seemed excited about something, the way he was moving his hands in the air."

"What was he wearing?"

"A blue coat. Dark blue. Made of sheepskin – the kind farmers wear. It's meant to be rainproof, you know?"

"What about the rest? His trousers and shoes? Any visible marks on his hands or face?"

"He wore glasses. And he had hair around the sides but not on top. Not sure about his trousers; I think they were dark. He had normal shoes on. Not trainers, I mean."

Kristy asked, "Have you seen him before?"

"I have, as it happens. He walks up and down this path, going towards the lock in the mornings. Mind you, a lot of people walk down the towpath in that direction. The bus stops just after the lock."

"Thank you. If you see this man again, be very careful. Don't speak to him. If he tries to sell you chocolates or cakes, avoid them."

The man's jaw went slack, then he licked his lips. "What's going on? What's he done?"

Nikki didn't see a reason to hide the truth anymore. "He's selling chocolates laced with poison. Please spread the word around. If you or your friends see him, call 999 and ask for the police immediately."

Nikki thanked the man and stepped off the houseboat. She walked rapidly towards the lock, Kristy by her side. The lock master wasn't at his station and his door was locked. Peering inside, Nikki saw a desk and leather chair, with TV screens on the wall.

"Can I help you?" a voice said behind them.

"Are you the lock master?" Nikki asked.

"Yes." His searching eyes looked Nikki and Kristy up and down. "You're not the detectives, are you? I heard they're looking for someone on the High Street. This old chap with a beard."

"Yes, have you seen him around?"

The lock master shrugged. "I see a lot of people come and go. To be honest, I've not really paid attention."

Kristy produced a photo of Fiona. "Have you seen this girl around? She came into Iffley yesterday and walked down here to the High Street."

The man looked carefully at the photo, then shook his head. "Sorry, I can't help you. But I can ask around. You want to find this old man? What for?"

"He's been selling poisoned chocolates. Two young women have died as a result."

The man's eyebrows shot up. "Is this the college student who fell from the walls? I heard about that."

Word spreads fast, Nikki thought. They still hadn't done a press conference about Chloe.

"Yes," she said. "If you see anyone matching the description of this old man, please get in touch with us. We'll be putting up e-fit photos everywhere."

"Some of the stall keepers remembered him," Monty said when Nikki and Kristy returned to the market and they walked towards the street where the old man had been seen. "He was new, and he kept to himself. Didn't speak much. He set up his stall and stayed inside. No one really spoke to him."

"He needed permission to set up that stall, didn't he?" Nikki asked.

Monty nodded. "Yes, from the Iffley market commission. Nish got in touch with them. They're looking through their records of recent entrants. There are quite a few, as the farmers come and go. We should have a list soon."

"Did the stall keepers mention what he sold?"

"Apparently, he barely had any business. He sold antiques and bric-a-brac that looked like it was from a car boot sale. Basically, all sorts. One of the farmer's assistants, a young woman, mentioned she saw him hand out chocolates to a girl this morning. The description matched the old man's."

Nikki shuddered. She just hoped the old man hadn't succeeded in luring too many people into his evil lair.

Then that gnawing sensation returned to the edge of her mind, destroying her peace. Did the old man put that note in Chloe's pocket?

Ask DI Nikki Gill what happened.

Even now, the words remained shocking. "And this man knew Chloe's mother, Connie" Nikki murmured, her eyes on the ground as they trudged up the gentle slope.

"Yes. He also told Chloe something that made her visit that hill where Connie was last seen. I can't help thinking this man had something to do with Connie's death," Monty mused.

Nikki looked up at him. She had been thinking along the same lines. However, they had no evidence so far. Jeffrey Pierson and Angela had both denied knowing anything. But Connie could have kept the man's identity a secret from Jeffrey. She could have been having an affair with him. Things soured, and the man then took his revenge...

Two uniformed constables stood guard at the mouth of a

quiet street lined with well-kept terraced houses. Kristy emerged and hurried over to Nikki and Monty. "We've got a breakthrough," she said, her eyes shining.

FORTY-FOUR

"A couple of the neighbours mentioned an old man who moved in a few months ago. Apparently, an elderly lady used to live in that house. She died, and he moved in. They think he's a relative, maybe her son, but they don't know for sure."

Kristy led Nikki and Monty to a house where two women were speaking to a uniformed constable. One of the women, who had a toddler in her arms, indicated the house opposite. "Old Mrs Pugh used to live there. She was almost a hundred years old, wasn't she?" She looked at the woman next to her.

This woman had her hair up in curlers, wore a dressing gown, and was smoking a cigarette. She took a long drag on it, then blew smoke out. "Yes. I think she hit a century this year. She got a letter from the king."

"Did you know her?" Nikki asked, introducing herself to them.

Both women shrugged. "She'd been around forever," the woman with the cigarette said. "I've lived here for ten years; I used to see her pottering around in the front garden. She stopped a couple of years ago. I think she became housebound.

Carers came from the council. Ambulances took her away to hospital a couple of times. She was a nice lady."

"When did you last see her?"

The two women looked at each other. The woman with the cigarette, who was older, spoke again. "A good few months, I'd say. Like I said, she didn't come out anymore. Then this old guy moved in. I think he was her son. He wasn't very friendly. Didn't talk to us much."

"Can you describe him?"

"He wasn't very tall. His hair had gone white. He was mostly bald. He wore this blue coat. I think he was in his sixties..." The woman took another deep drag of her cigarette.

The baby cried, and his mother shushed him. "I saw him a couple of times. He didn't come out much, to be honest. Not sure if he went out shopping or did things at night. And there were two people living there, I think..." She glanced at her friend, who nodded. "Yes, the older man with the beard."

Nikki narrowed her eyes at the cigarette smoker. "The other man didn't have a beard?"

Both women shook their heads. "The clean-shaven man arrived about a month ago. I'm not sure when the older guy arrived. But I saw more of him, to be honest."

"Can you describe them?" Nikki asked, exchanging a glance with Monty.

"Yes, he had a white beard and he wore a long blue coat. The weatherproof type. He also had glasses on. And he wore a black, peaked farmer's hat."

The smoker added her agreement. "Yes, I saw the old man as well. They were living in the same house. Mind you, both of them were about the same age, but the bearded man was slightly older. I think so, anyway..."

"Who arrived first?" Monty asked. "The clean-shaven man or the bearded one?"

The two women looked at each other. The smoker said,

"The clean-shaven man, definitely. He arrived a few months ago. I saw him speaking to the ambulance people when they took Mrs Pugh away. That was the last time we saw her. She was on a stretcher." She shrugged.

"Neither of you spoke to the men who moved in?" Nikki asked.

"No. They weren't very friendly, to be honest. Like I said, we mostly saw the bearded man. He left the house in the morning and came and went a few times. I think he had a stall in the market, didn't he?"

"Yes, Mandy next door saw him there. He was selling antique stuff. He didn't have much business. She didn't speak to him."

The smoker looked curiously at Nikki. "What's he done? The police have shut down the market as well, haven't they?"

When Nikki told them, both women gasped, their faces in shock.

"We'll know more as we dig into his background," Nikki said. "For now, please let everyone know: don't eat any chocolate that came from the market, just to be on the safe side."

They walked away, but the smoker called them back. "You know what," she said, coming up to Nikki. "There was this young lass who was asking about the man who lives in that house. She was a student, doing some sort of survey. She showed me her badge, and all. Damned if I can remember her name though. Carly, or something—"

"Chloe?"

The woman's eyes brightened. "That's it. Chloe. Her last name began with P. Parsons? Sorry, I'm just bollocks with names. She grinned, showing her yellow teeth.

"Pierson," Nikki said, glancing at Monty, who met her eyes. "When did you see her?"

"First time, a couple of months ago, I reckon. Recently, a couple of days ago."

"Okay, thanks. We might need to speak to you again, is that okay?"

"Sure."

"He definitely lived here, guv. Five of the neighbours saw him," the uniformed constable standing by Mrs Pugh's front door said as Nikki and Monty approached from across the road. "We opened the door and had a quick look inside. Nothing suspicious, but we didn't do a proper search."

The entrance hallway was narrow, with two doors leading off it, a living room and a kitchen at the back, and, between them, a staircase leading upstairs. Through the kitchen window, an overgrown garden was visible.

The living room's dark green wallpaper, which made the room look smaller than it was, was peeling in places. The two leather sofas were past their sell-by date, one of them with a broken armrest. Nikki went over to the bay window and parted the curtains.

An old TV stood in the corner, bookshelves on either side. Nikki picked up a framed photo from the bookshelf. It showed a woman in a wheelchair, with a man pushing her. They were by the seaside, and both were smiling for the camera. The man was clean-shaven, slim and of average height. He had brown hair, and as Nikki stared at him, the sudden shock of realisation hit her like a cannonball to the chest. She staggered back and bumped into Monty. She would have dropped the frame if Monty hadn't grabbed it.

"I've seen that guy before," Nikki whispered. Suddenly, flashes of lightning exposed the dark areas in her mind, synapses forming, illuminating areas she hadn't seen. She gasped, her eyes bulging with shock.

"John Lynes," she said, looking up at Monty. A hollow emptiness was spreading across her chest, and her lungs felt tight. She couldn't breathe. "The groundsman at New College." Shockwaves were rippling across her mind. Now she knew why the intruder at her house had looked familiar. *That lopsided left foot limp*. She had seen it in the groundsman as he walked away.

"My god," she gasped, putting a hand to her head. "He came to my house. I saw him in the garden."

"You sure?" Monty out a hand to her shoulder, steadying her. He lifted the framed photo so they could both see. "You think it's him?"

"Yes, I'm pretty sure."

Monty checked his phone. "I'm going to ask the lads to call the college and put out an all-points bulletin for him."

He ran outside and Nikki was left alone. Revelations whispered in her mind, dark voices she couldn't ignore.

Yes, it was him. In the darkness of the garden, she had still recognised his body shape. And the way he had walked off, with that left-sided limp.

She looked at the photo again. He had stubble on his cheeks, like he had when she first questioned him. The man who found the body. He'd have had enough time to put the note in Chloe's pocket.

Nikki closed her eyes. She should've suspected him right from the start.

What did John have against her? He was the one who had followed Fiona back to Cowley. Fiona had visited his stall.

Nikki heard footsteps, then Monty appeared. He held up the framed photo. "That's the man the neighbours saw arriving here a few months ago – the old lady's son, Steven Pugh."

Nikki was still gasping, her heart knocking loudly against her ribs. "But who was the old guy with the beard?' She locked eyes with Monty, realisation dawning. "Do you think it was Steven, in disguise?"

"They were never seen together. A beard and hat are easy to put on. And the glasses."

"So John Lynes is Steven Pugh?" Nikki asked the question. Monty inclined his head, a grim look on his face.

"Yes," he said. "I've already told the lads that. It has to be right?" He pointed at the framed photo of the man pushing the old woman in the wheelchair.

"This photo isn't that old. The similarity is obvious."

Rita nodded, still trying to control her surging pulse rate, and failing. Questions came and went like wind rushing through the trees.

"Let's finish checking out the place," Monty suggested.

The kitchen was clean, but had been used recently: the rubbish bin was half full and a plate with cutlery rested in the sink. Monty put the cutlery in an evidence bag.

After searching the room fully, they made their way into the narrow corridor. Monty suddenly stopped and put his hand on the door under the staircase, turning the handle, but nothing happened. He shook the handle, and still it didn't open. He looked at Nikki.

"This could be the basement. We need to get in."

"Knock it down," Nikki instructed urgently. Monty kicked the door, and it wobbled. He took two steps back and kicked again with all his might. The lock smashed and the door slammed open, knocking against the wall. Steps led into the darkness below. Monty ran his hand along the wall inside and as his fingers found the switch, a cone of yellow light appeared on the ceiling.

FORTY-FIVE

The small, dank basement had been turned into a kitchen – or more precisely, a chemist's laboratory set up. An electric hob stood in one corner and, on a desk, there were Bunsen burners, pipettes in their holders and another small electric hob with a pan on it.

Nikki gagged. A distinct, strange odour overpowered the closed air of the basement.

"Put your mask on – and don't touch anything," Monty warned.

Gingerly, he lifted the lid of the pan on the hob. He kept his face averted and looked from an angle. Nikki joined him. It was a brown liquid, which she easily recognised.

"Cocoa flakes, melted." Her eyes fell on the desk. Next to the Bunsen burners, she saw four small, black jars labelled with single letters. She picked up the nearest one, labelled A. Monty took it from her hand.

"Allow me." He turned around, and all she could see was his broad back. He shook the jar lightly, but no sound was audible. No powder inside.

Monty put the jar on the table, stepped back and Nikki saw a white coloured paste inside.

"Ayahuasca?" she whispered.

He picked up the next jar, which was labelled S. This one contained a powder.

"Scopolamine?" He raised an eyebrow.

"I guess we need to send everything to the lab. Hetty and Sheila will have a field day in here. I'll call Hetty. She needs to prioritise this."

Monty took out his torchlight and pointed it at the ground. The beam picked out a cardboard box with a lid on it. Slowly, as if there was a snake inside, Monty lifted the lid.

Inside were old chocolate trays – the sort that could be bought from supermarkets and given as gifts. Nikki's eyes widened as she stared at the logo.

Maxwell

Panic gripped Nikki. Her feet were rooted to the spot as her jaw dropped open. She bent over, as if punched in the guts. She had seen that chocolate tray before. In her mother's house. The tray dropped in through the letterbox. Clarissa's words floated in the musty air. *An old man with a beard has been walking around. Watching my house.*

"No..." Nikki whispered, breath struggling in her chest. Wave after wave of nausea crashing together in her stomach. She wanted to be sick.

The questions that had kicked up a storm in her mind were now answered.

Steven. She knew someone else by that name. Her mother's ex-partner. Tommy's father. The man who had made Clarissa into a heroin addict, then disappeared.

Nikki ran up the stairs, ignoring Monty's shouts behind her. She went out of the house, and staggered on the pavement, leaning against the wall. With cold fingers, she pulled out her phone. Clarissa didn't answer. She called twice, then rang the Thames Valley Police switchboard.

"DI Nikki Gill. Put me through to the duty uniforms team."

"Connecting. Hold on."

After a pause, a voice came on the line. "Hello guv, this is Sergeant Kilpatrick."

"Can you please dispatch a car to Clarissa Gill's home? She's my mother, and she's elderly, I'm concerned about her security. I want her picked up and taken to the South Kidlington nick."

"Sure, guv, no problem. Can you please send me your mother's address?"

Nikki did so, and Kilpatrick confirmed he would drive there himself.

She called Clarissa again but had no answer. She texted, a worry growing roots in her mind, dark tentacles unwinding in her heart. She told herself Clarissa was busy packing, chatting to the neighbours.

Monty met her in the corridor when she went back inside. "What's the matter?" He frowned. "You look pale."

"Tommy's father was called Steven. He was the heroin addict who got Mum into it. Good job he left... But now I think he's back – and has sent one of those packs of chocolate trays to my mum."

"What?" Concern creased Monty's features. "She didn't eat any, did she?"

"The tray was empty. I think he meant it as a warning. But it was one of those trays, I'm sure of it."

"Did you see photos of this Steven? Or know where he lived?"

"Mum showed me photos once. I never saw him, obviously. I can't remember his face well. He's a much older man now." The hollow space was spreading across Nikki's chest. She felt like she couldn't breathe. "He came back to Iffley, then got the groundsman job at New College."

"Fake papers? Or he changed his name?" Monty said, reaching for his phone.

"Maybe both."

Monty got in touch with Nish. He put Nish on the loudspeaker so Nikki could hear.

"John Lynes changed his name in 2015," Nish said. "I just spoke to the researchers. He was previously called Steven Pugh. His previous address was in Iffley, where you are now. As Steven Pugh, he had three PCNs for acting violently against a woman, and stalking."

"Well done," Nikki said, glancing at Monty. "Get as much detail on him as you can."

Nikki brushed past Monty and made for the stairs. "Let's finish here quickly. I need to get hold of Mum."

They went up the creaky stairs, the floor and landing covered in fading, threadbare green carpet.

Monty had to duck to enter the bathroom, while Nikki went into the first bedroom. The double bed had been slept in. She went to the bay window and flung the curtains open.

There was a desk with a laptop on it. She opened the drawers and found a zip-lock bag in one. She pulled it out and laid it on the bed. It was a large bag, and she unzipped it carefully.

Inside was a collection of fake beards, all different shades of white. Under the beards, there were three peaked farmer's hats, all in black. Next to them, two pairs of glasses rested inside their cases.

Monty came into the room and whistled. "So, that was his disguise. He lived a double life, didn't he? Part-time bearded farmer's market stall holder, and groundsman at New College the rest of the time."

Monty lifted out a shoebox and found a small, steel, black

box with a latch inside. The latch was old and rusty, and he had to fiddle with it before it opened. Inside, he found a collection of old photos.

Monty held one of the photos up to the light. It was a faded image, but Nikki recognised a much younger version of Clarissa.

A man, who resembled the person in the photo frame downstairs, stood next to her, holding a baby in his arms. They were both smiling proudly, and the summer sunshine cascaded over them. Nikki took the photo from Monty's hand.

She noted the baby's blond hair, and his chubby cheeks. He looked so cute. Monty passed her another photo, that of Clarissa with the baby on her lap.

"Tommy," Nikki whispered. The brother she had never known. A black weight lodged against her throat, spreading upwards, forcing moisture to her eyes. She found a tissue in her pocket and wiped her useless tears.

She slid against the wall to the floor, not caring if she disturbed evidence. The weight of everything they'd discovered had left her fractured, her mind dislocated.

Steven Pugh was Tommy's father. There was no doubt in her mind. And he was also responsible for Chloe's— Nikki's eyes widened. How had Steven known Connie? Jeffrey had told her they lived in Wolvercote then, just up the road from Jericho, where Clarissa had lived.

Monty extended his hand. She took it and got to her feet. She told him where Connie had lived before she disappeared.

"Very close to your mother... Do you think Clarissa might've known Connie?"

"I don't know. I need to speak to my mum."

Nikki's phone rang and she answered. It was Sergeant Kilpatrick. He sounded apologetic. "I'm sorry, guv, but your mother's not around. The door's locked and she's not answering."

The worry was now cascading down Nikki's spine, sending shockwaves to her limbs. Her pulse rate was booming in her ears, her mouth dry. "I told her not to leave the house. Can you please look in the garden?"

"You want me to go over the side gate?"

"Yes. And if she's not there, speak to the neighbours opposite and on each side. She must be somewhere close. Call me back."

Monty looked at her questioningly.

"I can't find my mum," Nikki said, the panic now numbing her heart. Monty gripped her shoulders and she touched his hand. Her head dropped as she breathed heavily. She needed to stay in control.

"Let's go find her," Monty said. "Come on."

Downstairs, as they finished up their search, Nikki's phone rang again.

"Guv, it's Kilpatrick here. Your mother's not in the garden. One of the neighbours saw a man go inside her house, a little while ago. The neighbour describes him as an older man, wearing a blue coat. Your mother let him in."

"What? When did this happen?" Nikki gasped.

"About fifteen minutes before we turned up, according to the neighbour. She was watching through the window. She saw the man help your mother load her suitcase in the car."

Nikki thought quickly. Clarissa's street had CCTV.

"What sort of a car was it?"

"A black Ford Focus, according to the neighbour. Why would this man pick up your mum?"

"Because he's got a vendetta against me and my family. He killed those girls. He's now abducted my mum. Inform all units. Get that car's registration number. I want live ANPR right now. I'll meet you at the scene."

FORTY-SIX

"Steven, stop the car!" Clarissa cried out. Her voice was hoarse and her heart thudded against her ribs. Sweat caked her forehead, plastering her hair to her skin. "Please, stop."

Steven didn't answer. His jaw was clenched tight and a muscle twitched on his temple. Clarissa had pleaded with him and tried to grab his shoulder, but he had flung her hand away.

"Do you want to see your daughter die?" he said, looking at her in the rearview mirror.

Clarissa shrank back in her seat, her eyes bulging with fear. "Why would you do that?"

"You and Nikki went on to have a great life, didn't you? You cut me loose without caring what happened to me. I didn't get to see my son. You took him away from me."

"No," Clarissa cried, pounding her fists on her legs. "That's not true, and you know it." Her voice shook. "They took Tommy away from me. They said I couldn't raise him. I told you what happened."

"But you didn't call me for help. I could have got Tommy back."

"Help?" Clarissa was aghast, despite the dire situation. "It was you who got me into that mess in the first place! You injected me with that horrible crap and turned my life into a nightmare. Why would I want you around?"

"Because I could have helped you. I wouldn't have let them take Tommy away."

"There was nothing you could have done." Clarissa covered her face with her hands. "Look, it's all in the past now. Why are you doing this? Where are you taking me? Steven, please. Nikki will be looking for me."

Steven was silent again. When his eyes were fully on the road and she thought he wouldn't notice, making as little movement as possible, she searched through her pockets again and looked inside her coat, knowing she wouldn't find her phone. Then, her fingers closed around something else: a pen.

"I need to wee," she told him. His eyes flicked to the rearview mirror, then back to the road again.

"Please, I'm bursting."

"No," he said gruffly. "Pee in your pants if you have to."

Clarissa knew he was trying to put as much distance between himself and Oxford as possible.

She glanced at the other cars on the road. Even if she tried to signal for help, they wouldn't notice and it would only make him even angrier.

She had to do something. She took out the pen and gripped it in her hand.

"Did you send me that box of chocolates?" she asked.

Steven glanced at the rearview mirror again, holding her gaze for a fraction longer.

"Yes."

"Why?" She needed to keep him talking.

"I wanted you to try one. But I didn't send any. That was going to come a few days later. Then I realised I wanted to see you. I wanted you to know what you've done to me."

"I did nothing to you. You destroyed my life. If you had stayed around, you would have destroyed Tommy as well. What sort of father would you have been?" Clarissa raised her voice in a mocking tone. "I'm glad you left." She leaned forward, trying to distract his attention from the road.

"You know what you are? A coward. You never had the guts to face your responsibilities. You injected heroin so you could hide from the world. You never did an honest day's work in your life."

She could see his face reddening with anger. He spoke through clenched teeth. "Shut up."

"Look at what you're doing now," she snorted. She held the pen tightly in her right hand, hiding it from Steven's view. "You're abducting an innocent pensioner. How do you think that's going to look in the newspapers? Will they give you a medal or throw you in prison?

"You're a joke." She laughed loudly. "A miserable worm who should crawl back into the hole you emerged from. You're not even a human being. I'm glad Tommy never got to know you."

"Shut up!" Steven screamed, his cheeks now flushed as he breathed heavily. The car swerved dangerously, forcing him to slow down. Other cars honked, and Steven gritted his teeth, cursing. Clarissa grabbed her chance.

She was now leaning forward between the seats and as she raised herself up on her legs, she lashed her right arm out. She thrust the pen into his left eye and he howled in agony. He slammed on the brakes, and his left hand came off the steering wheel as he desperately tried to straighten the car.

The rear fishtailed, and the car went into a spin onto the hard shoulder. Steven clasped one hand over his bleeding left eye and tried to control the car with the other, but he couldn't stop it swerving.

The car hit the steel fence on the left of the hard shoulder and Clarissa was thrown to one side. Her head smashed against the window glass as it shattered, fragments of glass showering over her head as she curled up into a foetal position on the seat.

FORTY-SEVEN

Clarissa's head was spinning and there was a loud ringing sound in her ears. The light swam in her eyes, and she couldn't focus. She lifted her head, and a fireball of pain ignited in the back of her skull. She winced and leaned against the seat.

From the corner of her eye, she saw cars moving by on the road to her right. The driver's seat was empty and the door was open. Before she could move, she saw Steven. He rose up from the ground like an apparition, hand clasping a tissue over his left eye. The tissue was stained red.

Clarissa shrank back in fear as he approached and yanked the rear door open. He reached in, hands groping for her. Clarissa kicked with her legs, hitting Steven in the face. He howled in agony. Moving fast, she opened Frodo's cage and he leaped out. As Steven reached for her again, the cat bit Steven's hand. The man cursed, swiping at Frodo.

Undaunted, Steven reached for Clarissa again. She kicked with her legs again and managed to hit him in the face. He stumbled back and flopped down on the hard shoulder of the motorway.

Cars roared and zoomed past. A truck went by, covering

them with dust and exhaust fumes. Clarissa coughed, hand over her mouth. Then she managed to get into the front seat. She took the car keys and searched in the dashboard but couldn't find her phone. She got out of the car. Steven was getting to his feet slowly. Blood caked the left side of his face. He stood there, panting. Then he moved towards her.

Clarissa backed away, and realised she had to make a run for it. But her legs were tired, and although she was able to walk around, courtesy of both knees being replaced, she couldn't run. Steven stumbled behind her, and he was faster. He caught up with her, just as another car pulled up ahead. A man got out and ran over to her.

"Help me," Clarissa gasped and sobbed. "He's trying to kill me." The man held her up as she collapsed.

"Let her go," Steven shouted above the din of the motorway. "She's my wife."

"No, I'm not!"

Steven came forward and the man shielded Clarissa behind his back. "Go and sit in the car," he said, but Clarissa didn't. Her head was throbbing, and her eyes swam. She had to focus with an effort. She stepped out from behind the man and approached Steven.

"Why did you come back?"

"I told you. My mother died. I came back, and realised while my mother had died, Connie's daughter, and your daughter, were still alive."

"Who?"

"Your friend in Wolvercote, Constance."

Clarissa frowned, shaking her head. Steven bared his teeth in a smile. "Your friend, Connie. The quiet one. Small and blonde. She had mental health problems. Remember her?"

A distant memory flared to life in Clarissa's tired mind. "Connie? But she..." A sudden realisation convulsed Clarissa, like she was spinning around in a washing machine.

"Connie disappeared." Clarissa pointed a finger at Steven. "That was you? You did that to her?"

Steven didn't speak. He stopped and stared at her.

"First Chloe, then Nikki. I wanted to bring Nikki down. Instead of poisoning her, I chose to destroy her career." He snarled then, and it was like seeing a hyena open its mouth. "But she came after me. That's when I knew I should've finished you before I killed her."

Steven lunged for her, but she moved away and the stranger stepped in between them. Sirens got louder, and within seconds, two police cars pulled up on the hard shoulder, blue lights blazing.

Nikki jumped out of the first car and ran over to them. Two uniformed officers helped handcuff Steven and kept him on the ground. Clarissa fell into Nikki's hug, weeping.

"It's my fault," she sobbed. "I did this to you. To everyone. It's my fault."

Nikki pressed her harder and whispered in her ears. "It's okay, Mum. It's alright, I'm here now."

FORTY-EIGHT

The late afternoon sunlight slanted in through the windows of Clarissa's house. Nikki observed her mother. She had two stitches on her forehead and was now resting on the sofa with her feet up. Clarissa had been quiet since she'd returned back home.

"Grandma," Rita called out from the kitchen, "you don't take sugar, do you?" The teenager's arrival had lifted their spirits considerably.

"No, just some milk. And get me a couple of those chocolate biscuits."

"Okay. Mum, do you want a biscuit as well?"

What the hell, why not, Nikki thought. "Yes, get me a couple." She glanced at her mother. "Mum, are you okay? Did you take the painkillers this morning?"

Clarissa shook her head. "It only hurts when I touch it. I'm all right." She held Nikki's gaze for a few seconds.

Nikki was concerned. Her mother had stayed in hospital overnight and come home that morning. Her head scan was clear, and she had no other injuries. But Nikki knew the real scars would be hidden. After all, it was Steven, the father of

Tommy, who had tipped Clarissa into depression and heartbreak. After what happened to Tommy, Nikki's relationship with her mother had deteriorated, partly due to Clarissa's alcoholism. Now, with Rita, their relationship was back on track, and Nikki knew she'd have to keep a close eye on her mother.

Steven was in custody, and there was enough evidence to convict him for the murders of Chloe and Fiona. Thankfully, he would spend the rest of his days in prison.

"Do me a favour, darling," Clarissa said to Rita after the teenager had put the tray down on the coffee table. "See that photo album on the shelf? The red and yellow one." Clarissa pointed.

Rita nodded and crossed the room. She stood on her tiptoes and retrieved the album.

Clarissa sat up and slowly flicked through the pages. Nikki watched her, aware of what she was doing.

"Mum," she said softly. "Leave it alone."

Clarissa looked up at her. "I want you to see this."

"I've seen the photos before," Nikki said gently. They were photos of Steven and her half-brother, Tommy. She hadn't told her mother about the photos Steven had in his possession. They were now with the forensics department.

Clarissa's eyes flickered down to the old photo album. "I can't believe he came back after all these years," she whispered.

"His mother died," Nikki said. "He got himself the groundsman job at New College with his new identity. He saw me at a press conference for a case, a few months ago. I think he also saw me at New College when I volunteered there for security. That's how he found out I was in Thames Valley Police. My ID would've been registered in the porters' lodge."

Nikki, like a few senior members of the TVP, had permission to attend mass and choir at Oxford colleges' chapels. They also volunteered their services, helping out the college's security staff.

Nikki lapsed into silence and shook her head. Then she got up and gently prised the album from Clarissa's hands. The older woman resisted at first, then gave up. Nikki sat down next to her mother and put a hand on her arm.

"It's not your fault. He was an evil man, and you did the right thing by getting rid of him." Nikki exhaled. "We found Connie's body buried beside a derelict cottage on Blenheim Hill – Steven gave us the location. DNA and dental records have identified her. She can finally be laid to rest."

Nikki thought back to what Chloe and Jeff had endured all these years – the pain, the lack of closure. An endless chasm that Chloe would never be able to bridge now that she was gone, but at least Jeff could, on his daughter's behalf. But his loss was doubled now, and far greater.

Nikki looked at Clarissa and realised how grateful she was that her mother was alive and well, and had come out of this ordeal relatively unscathed. She would always remain close to Clarissa, never let her come in harm's way again.

Tears welled in Clarissa's eyes. "Chloe never got to see her mother's grave..."

"Yes. But she was a brave girl. She tried her best." Nikki paused. "Steven also confessed to the murders of two other women in 2009 and 2011 – he took them to Blenheim Hills too."

They sat in silence for a while, sipping their tea. Rita asked, "Who were they, these women?"

"There's no match on their DNA profiles on our police records. Dental records are still being searched. It's possible these women were homeless, or sex workers. They might also have been drug addicts. No one reported them missing."

Clarissa started to weep, and Rita came over and put an arm around her grandmother's shoulder. They sat in silence, the three guardians of a terrible truth that had claimed so many innocent lives.

"It's all over now," Nikki said. "We can move on with our lives." She pressed Clarissa's hand, feeling the wrinkled, gnarly skin, smoothing the spots on the hand gently with her thumb. "He'll never come back again, Mum. You know that, don't you?"

"Yes, I suppose so," Clarissa sighed. Nikki held her hand, hoping her mother wouldn't be left with any enduring emotional scars.

"We're here, Mum," she said encouragingly. Clarissa looked at her, gripped her hand tighter, and then smiled at her and Rita.

FORTY-NINE

A grey sky hung heavy over the cemetery as the mourners stood in hushed silence around Chloe's grave. Meagre moments of sun filtered through, casting light on the coffin as if to commemorate the young life they were celebrating.

"Dearly beloved, we are gathered here today..." The vicar gently raised his voice as he gave his sermon.

Nikki cast her eyes to Jeffrey Pierson, who stood with hands folded, head bowed. Grief lined his face, and his eyes were shut, but his lips moved, as if he was praying, atoning for the remorse of his sins.

The vicar finished his service. Jeffrey and Angela solemnly threw flowers on the coffin as it was lowered into the grave.

Nikki couldn't bear to watch, her heart breaking for Jeffrey. Tears budded in her eyes, and she wiped them away with a tissue.

Slowly, the gathering filtered out of the silent graveyard to make their way to the wake at a pub nearby. Both Nikki and Monty were invited. They caught up with Jeff as he said goodbye to someone. He was emotional when he saw Nikki.

"My brave little girl did what I couldn't," Jeffrey said, the words catching in his throat. He seemed to have aged decades in the last few days. Angela gripped his arm, almost holding him up straight. "She tracked down Steven. Why didn't she ask for help?"

"She didn't know what it would lead to. She felt she had to do this on her own. Her personal search for what happened to her mother."

They walked slowly to the car park. Nikki asked, "Did you find the notebook?"

Angela answered. "Yes. It was in her room, in the desk drawer."

Nikki nodded. That was why they didn't find it in Chloe's room at New College.

"Fiona's father called me," Jeffrey said. "We're meeting up tomorrow." He glanced at Nikki. "What going to happen to Steven?"

"He's going to stand trial. He's confessed already. Then he's going to rot in jail for the rest of his life."

"He deserves to die," Jeffrey ground the words out. "How can an evil man like him be allowed to live when my beautiful little girl is dead?"

"You should take some time off. Go somewhere," Monty suggested. "Nothing will help to ease the pain, but a change of scenery might help."

"Yes," Angela agreed. "That's what we will do."

They stopped in front of Monty's car. Jeffrey shook Nikki's hand and his face crumpled. Nikki pulled him into a hug, and she felt her own tears.

"I'm sorry," she whispered.

"No, thank you..." Jeffrey said. "Without you, I would never have known what happened to Connie, and of course, Chloe." He smiled sadly. "I will always remember you, Nikki."

A LETTER FROM THE AUTHOR

Dear Reader,

I hope you enjoyed *Fatal Secret*, the third book in my Detective Nikki Gill series.

If you'd like to join other readers in keeping in touch, here are two options. Stay in the loop with my new releases with the link below. You'll be the first to know about all future books I write. Or sign up to my personal email newsletter on the link at the bottom of this note. You'll get bonus content and get occasional updates and insights from my writing life. I'd be delighted if you choose to sign up to either – or both!

www.stormpublishing.co/ml-rose

If you enjoyed *Fatal Secret* and could spare a few moments to leave a review that would be hugely appreciated. Even a short review can make all the difference in encouraging a reader to discover my books for the first time. Thank you so much!

Join other readers in hearing about my writing (and life) experience, and other bonus content. Simply head over to www.BookHip.com/VKKKXJB

When I spent time in Oxford, my friends told me about a student who was admitted to hospital with drug poisoning – but the actual chemical was a strange cocktail of various substances. That got me thinking – what if a chemical like that spread amongst the student population? Then I thought of Nikki's brother, Tommy's father... and suddenly, a plot had formed. From there on, the story took a life of itself. I enjoyed creating Steven Pugh's character. He's really evil, and very resourceful. But he met his match in Clarissa, who took the fight to him.

I would like to thank my editor, Claire Bord, for the brainstorming sessions. Claire has been with Nikki from day one, helping me bringing her to life.

Also thanks to the copyeditor, Natasha Hodgson, and the proofreader, Abigail Fenton, without whom this book wouldn't be complete. And Alexandra Begley, for being patient with me while I was a few thousand miles away from my desk.

To the entire production and marketing team at Storm who work behind the scenes – thanks for all you do to make the books find a place in our reader's hearts.

I hope you enjoyed reading Nikki's latest case. If you did, please leave a review; they take two minutes of your time, but guide other readers forever.

Thank you for reading,

M.L. Rose

facebook.com/arlabake

Printed in Dunstable, United Kingdom